Mariposa Gown

Also by **Rigoberto González**

Black Blossoms (2011)

Camino del Sol: Fifteen Years of Latina and Latino Writing (editor) (2010)

The Mariposa Club (2009)

Men without Bliss (2008)

Butterfly Boy: Memories of a Chicano Mariposa (2006)

Other Fugitives and Other Strangers (2006)

Antonio's Card (2005)

Crossing Vines (2003)

Soledad Sigh-Sighs (2003)

So Often the Pitcher Goes to Water until It Breaks (1999)

Mariposa Gown

Rigoberto González

Tincture
an IMPRINT OF LETHE PRESS

Published in 2012 by TINCTURE, an imprint of
LETHE PRESS, INC.
118 Heritage Avenue • Maple Shade, NJ 08052-3018
www.lethepressbooks.com • lethepress@aol.com
ISBN: 1-59021-351-3
ISBN-13: 978-1-59021-351-3

Set in Minion, Marker Felt, and Market.
Interior and cover design: Alex Jeffers.
Interior illustrations: iStockphoto.com.
Author photo: Deidre Schoo.
Cover photo: © Monart Design - Fotolia.com.
Gown and corsage: Peachboy Distillery & Design.

LIBRARY OF CONGRESS CATALOGING-IN-PUBLICATION DATA
González, Rigoberto.
Mariposa gown / Rigoberto González.
p. cm.
Summary: Caliente Valley High School senior Maui, a gay Latino, is torn between his growing affection for a wealthy newcomer and his loyalty to the GLBT alliance he helped found, whose members consider making a statement by attending prom in drag.
ISBN 978-1-59021-351-3 (pbk. : alk. paper)
[1. Gays--Fiction. 2. High schools--Fiction. 3. Schools--Fiction. 4. Mexican Americans--Fiction. 5. Gay-straight alliances in schools--Fiction. 6. Clubs--Fiction] I. Title.
PZ7.G594Sep2012 [Fic]--dc22
2011034639

in memoriam

Carl Walker-Hoover and Jaheem Herrera

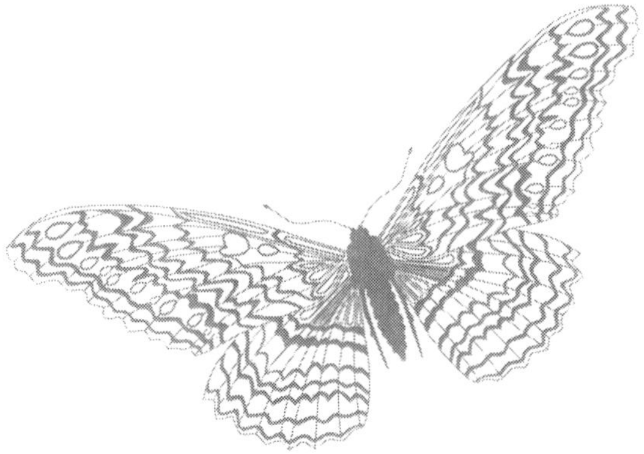

PART ONE

January Jeer, February Fierceness

The Fierce Trio

These are a few of my favorite (Christmas) things: a second-hand man-purse from Trini, an impressive homemade Gothic skeleton ballerina in a red lace tutu from Lib, a gift certificate to Footlocker from Papi, a selection of generic-brand underwear and socks from Mickey, a cool cap with a small black butterfly stitched on the side from Celie, and a nice contribution to the college fund from Mr. Dutton. This last one came in the form of an apology since Joyería Dutton had officially closed its display cases by New Year's, as did many of the stores in Lame View Mall. It wasn't that shooting incident during the Christmas season that did it, it was a much more all-consuming bullet—the economy. Caliente Valley, like every other working-class community in the nation, didn't weather the storm without casualties, and Joyería Dutton was one of them. And even though I'm sad to see Mr. Dutton and his entire brood of girls pack up and leave our valley for greener pastures in LA county, I suspect this move is also an effort by the Dutton family to get closer to Isaac.

Isaac I don't hear from at all—not a phone call, not an email—but I have learned to let it go. The Fierce Foursome has long ago been reduced to a Trio.

I'm sitting at the dining room table with my eyes glued to Mr. Dutton's shaky signature in blue ink on the check when Papi walks up behind me and puts his hand on my shoulder.

"Would you like to come work for me?" he says.

"Washing dishes?" I ask, remembering that this was once my punishment for getting detention from high school. I suppose getting paid for it won't be so bad.

"You know," Papi says, "dishwashing is an honest job, but I've got plenty of guys who want to work their way up to server at the restaurant. I was thinking you could help Yolanda host. I think she's eventually going to shift full time to her second job, which pays better. I don't blame her, not in these times."

I weigh my options: smiling at the entrance of Las Cazuelas for minimum wage or pouting at home for free.

"What kind of clothes will I have to wear?" I say. Yolanda always looks so pretty in her señorita outfit, but somehow I don't think cross-dressing is suddenly acceptable in the place that Trini scandalized when she wore the ballet folklórico dress at the annual banquet of the Latino Chamber of Commerce.

Papi chuckles. It's a nervous laugh that tells me he's remembering the same thing. "We have the regulation shirts," he says. "I think you'll look great in a guayabera."

A guayabera—a Mexican wedding shirt with multiple pockets and an embroidery of flowers. *Très* ethnic.

"When do I start?" I say.

"How about on January sixth?" Papi says.

Día de los Reyes Magos—Three Kings Day—the day the baby Jesus receives his gold, frankincense and myrrh. How appropriate, since employment is yet another one of Papi's gifts to me. And since I don't really need the lay of the land, I can jump right into the guacamole bowl on the first busy night of a Mexican restaurant's winter season. I can already hear the girls as I pick up the phone to call a special sleepover on the last weekend before school starts.

"I think it's inspired of your father to bring in a literal Mary to greet the visitors to the manger," Trini says from the couch as she applies a fresh coat of pink to her toenails. I'm amazed that Trini hasn't changed one bit over the holidays. She's still thin and petite, unlike Lib and me who have packed on a few pounds, though it's not as visible on me because I've grown a few inches since last summer. Lib hides it beneath his black Goth attire—coats and vests—but I can tell from his face that he's heavier. Still, I think they're both adorable.

Lib rolls his eyes. We're making the ham and cheese sandwiches in the kitchen.

"Well, congrats, Maui," Lib says. "I think you'll be a *fabulous* hostess—you've got perfect white teeth, a twinkle in your eye and a lovely expression on your face that says: *Eat here and, please, don't forget your gas pills.*"

"You two are terrible," I say, laughing.

"Just kidding," Lib says. "It'll be fine! It'll be great. And let me know if there are any other openings. I'm keeping my eye out for some extra income myself." Lib suddenly stops and turns to Trini: "And one word out of you, Miss Sassy, about me being part of the menagerie and I'll kick the nail polish off your feet!"

"What? Me?" Trini says, clutching imaginary pearls. "Girl, I'm feeling the hard times myself. Why do you think I get to come here instead of staying home with Aunt Carmen? My mother has been spending more and more time at the house since she lost her job. I hope she and my father aren't planning something sneaky."

"Like what?" I ask. Lib and I make our way to the living room with the tray of munchies.

"I don't know," Trini says. "Maybe moving Aunt Carmen to a home and renting out her house. Then I'd have to move back in with you, Passion Flower." Trini bats her eyelashes at me.

"Maui's father runs a Mexican restaurant, not a homeless trannie shelter," Lib says.

"Oh, you hush, Vampira," Trini retorts. "Why don't you go sink your teeth into the tires of an ice cream truck?"

"And why don't *you* go overdose on your acetone?" Lib answers back.

"That's enough, girls," I say, sitting between them. "Washboard stomach ahoy."

That's enough to keep the peace for now. We snuggle in front of the television to watch our Ryan Reynolds movie marathon and squeal every time he happens to walk around without his shirt, which is often. But truth be told, I'm feeling distracted, thinking about how in just six months we grab our high school diplomas like lady fans, hike up our skirts and tiptoe forward into who knows what debutante ball. Lib had the brilliant idea of us applying to all the same colleges, though I think he'll have plenty more options than I will, and when the time comes, I'll convince him that it's okay if we go to different schools. As much as I like the thought of us sticking together for a while longer, I wouldn't want to hold him back. And I'm hoping that Trini will either enroll in community college or at least get her practicing license at a cosmetology school—anything but get into more trouble with losers like Davy Wavy. I shudder whenever I recall *that* mess.

Let me turn back instead to what matters: the Fierce Trio. My throat tightens every time I think about saying goodbye to these movie nights, to bidding adiós to the not-so-innocent and somewhat carefree adolescence, where hard lessons are usually followed by sentimental hugs and air kisses. Trini and Lib are my best friends, my extended family, and the ugly emptiness that will be my life without them within reach frightens me. I wrap my arms around them and squeeze our bodies together.

"Are you having a moment?" Trini says.

"Yeah, what brought this on?" Lib adds.

"Nothing," I say, slightly embarrassed. "I'm just happy we're together tonight, that's all. Are you girls coming to see me on my first night on the job?"

"Of course!" Trini says. "And then Las Cazuelas will be forced to call it Three Queens Day."

"I'll bake a cake," Lib says.

"Chocolate, my favorite," I say.

"Certainly not," Trini says. "There's only one kind worth bringing to celebrate anyone in the Mariposa Club."

"What?" I say, but only because I know what follows is the corny and predictable moment of bonding that reminds us that we're still allowed to be a little silly.

As if on cue, all three of us shout in unison: "Fruitcake!"

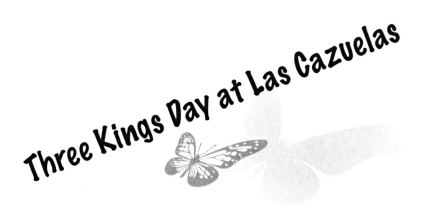

Three Kings Day at Las Cazuelas

I don my gay apparel—a slimming pearl-colored guayabera and a pair of linen pants—and take my place behind the hostess counter next to Yolanda.

"Thank goodness you're here," Yolanda says. "Now I can take my cigarette breaks."

"I didn't know you smoked?" I say.

"I don't," she says. "But the boss does. And he understands a cigarette break. A break to get on the cell phone and fight with my soon-to-be ex-boyfriend—*that* he doesn't get."

"Oh."

Yolanda pulls out a chart with a map to the restaurant and guides me through the how-to-keep-the-servers-happy-by-distributing-the-customers-evenly-at-all-the-stations process.

"The clipboard is for the unhappy people's waiting list, the lollipops are for the annoying toddlers and the business cards," she says as she flips one over, "are for writing down your number for the cute—" she stops at mid-sentence—"never mind."

She walks me through the chain of command without taking a breath: "Customers will bitch to the servers, servers will call for help to the host, the host determines whether or not it moves up to the manager (your papi), and then the manager takes over."

I nod.

"But try to resolve it if you can," Yolanda warns me. "The only things managers want to hear are compliments, not complaints. And never go straight to the boss, unless you've got problems with the manager, which I don't expect you will."

"I hope not."

"Other than that," Yolanda concludes, "just keep the K-Y handy."

I do a double take. "Excuse me?"

She pulls out a small tube from behind the counter, squeezes a bit on her index finger, and then rubs it across her teeth. "It's what keeps that smile winning."

"Gotcha," I say and nod.

Since I'll be here after school on weekdays, I'll be taking care of the late lunch and early dinner crowds. I'll have Saturdays off, but Sunday brunch is also mine, which means no sleeping in like I'm used to. I shadow Yolanda a few times to get a sense of the formality, and it's so fake it's easy to replicate: *Your server will be right with you! Enjoy your dinner! Nice tie! Don't choke on the chips, now, y'hear?* This last phrase, Yolanda explains, is reserved for the high blood pressure customers who get their panties in a bunch over a five-minute wait at the door.

"And you roll it around in your head until you're back at the greeting counter," Yolanda says. "It'll get you through a tough night."

"I must confess I didn't realize I had to be so quick to the wit to work at Las Cazuelas. I would've gotten a job here sooner," I tell Yolanda.

As Yolanda and I take our positions, Papi (who I have to refer to as Mr. Gutiérrez while on the job) and the boss/the owner/the stuffy old white guy in a suit walk through the door having such an intense conversation that they pass us by without even looking up to acknowledge our stupid smiles pasted across our faces. My father waves his fingers over his shoulder apologetically.

"That, in case you didn't know, is Mr. Benson," Yolanda says, keeping her smile intact. "You can call him Mr. Menso, but only after you've worked here at least two hours."

"Oh, my gosh," I say, keeping my smile intact as well. "This is just like high school."

"Keep your nose clean, kid. You might make class president."

The novelty of Three Kings Day at Las Cazuelas is that the three kitchen workers who lost the lottery have to dress up as royalty and pose for pictures with crying children all evening. It's the photograph in which no one looks happy. Yolanda and I take turns offering each child a consolation prize, their Three Kings Day gift: a coloring book and a box with five crayons. Yippee. For tonight, one of the private side rooms has been turned into a stable of some sort and a large stuffed camel that's seen better desert days stands at the center looking dejected that it has to withstand the weight of tiny kicking bodies. Papi explained that the side room was going to be turned into a Mexican curio market, and that eventually, if I wanted to I could work there as a sales representative. But why would I deny myself the chance to stand at the front door, receiving the hungry and the cranky for hours on end?

At about eight in the evening, Papi comes out to check up on me.

"Doing fine, Mr. Gutiérrez," I say.

"Good, good," he says. "Where's Yolanda?"

"On her cigarette break," I say.

"Oh," Papi says. "She should really just dump the guy. Anyway, listen carefully, Maui, we have a VIP coming in around this time—a Mr. Sandoval and his son. It's very important that you let me know as soon as you seat them because Mr. Benson and I have to come out to welcome them."

"The red carpet treatment, huh? What are they, politicians?"

"Almost," Papi says. "Mr. Sandoval is the owner of a construction company coming into town to clean things up under the county's new stimulus plan. It could mean the salvation of this valley. It's a point of pride for Mr. Benson to have Las Cazuelas be one of Mr. Sandoval's dining spots."

"Nice," I say.

"And one more thing, be kind to his son," Papi says before he flies back to his office. "He's going to be finishing up his senior year of high school here, so he'll be the new kid."

I roll my eyes. Oh, great. I can just imagine the nerdo who's going to be walking in through the door, and now I have to kiss his ass in school while my father kisses his father's ass at the restaurant. I look at my watch. Trini and Lib should have been here an hour ago. Only they can cheer me up now.

Yolanda comes back as she's slipping her cell phone into her purse. "What did I miss?"

"Nothing much," I say. "Except that King Sandoval and the Crown Prince are showing up here any minute."

"Are you kidding me?" Yolanda says, reaching up to fix her hair. "Do you realize who Francisco Sandoval is?"

"The owner of a construction company coming to save Caliente Valley?"

"And," Yolanda says, searching for her lipstick. "California's most eligible divorcé. He owns a vineyard in Napa Valley! Let me go fix my face, I'll be right back!"

"Geez," I say. "You too? I guess we'll have to pass out numbers to kiss Mr. Sandoval's ring."

A young couple comes in and asks for a private booth, so I comply, and by the time I get back to the counter, I know I'm in the presence of power. Mr. Sandoval is tall and distinguished looking, sporting expensive threads that are clearly in shock after having been paraded around in our working-class town all day.

"Good evening, sir," I say.

Mr. Sandoval shakes my hand and my knees go weak. Ooh la la, indeed, what a grip and what a gorgeous pair of green eyes. But before I have time to get to the next line on my script, Yolanda steps in and shoves me out of the way.

"I will be taking you to your seat this evening, Mr. Sandoval," she says.

"Lovely," Mr. Sandoval says. "My son Sebastián is in the men's room."

"Maui here can bring him right over," Yolanda says.

I blush. "Mauricio," I say.

"Well, thank you, Mauricio," Mr. Sandoval says as he follows Yolanda to the nicest table in the place, the one that doesn't face the kitchen.

"Good evening, handsome," I hear someone say, and when I turn around it's as if my head's been hit with a basketball because in front of me is none other than a younger, more delicate version of Mr. Sandoval, green eyes and all.

"Good evening to you too," I say, and then my mouth dries up. Did he just call me handsome?

"I'm Sebastián," he says and holds out his hand.

"I'm Maui, I mean, Mauricio, I mean—call me Maui. We're going to be school buddies."

"Oh, well I hope we will be much more than that," he says and my heart drops to my stomach. Is this some kind of big city flirting or what? I think I'm going to drool all over my guayabera.

"Yes, well, please follow me," I say. "Your father's already seated."

As we make our way to the dining room I can't help but feel Sebastián's eyes drilling holes into my backside. But thankfully the host has a small role to play (not that that has stopped Yolanda from overstaying her welcome at Mr. Sandoval's table) and I zip out to my father's office. Papi nearly trips over his chair on his way out to grab Mr. Benson. If tonight is any indication of what awaits us all, we're in deep nacho dip.

When I get back to the counter, there's Trini and Lib. Trini's wearing a fabulous pink polka-dot top, but looking distressed.

"What happened? Why are you girls like five hours late getting here?" I ask.

"Oh, wait until you hear this," Lib says.

Trini sobs into her hands. "My social life is over," she says.

"Wait," I say, and guide them over to the Three Kings Day photo-op room. The kings are done for the night. "What's going on?"

"I told you I suspected my parents were up to something," Trini says.

"Oh, shit," I say. "Don't tell me they're putting Aunt Carmen in a home and renting out her house?"

"Worse," Lib says. "They're renting out *their* house."

"What?" I say.

Trini nods her head. "Yes, they can charge more money if they rent out their own home, so they're moving in with Aunt Carmen and me."

"Now you see?" Lib says. "Trini and Trini's father? Vinegar and oil?"

"Well, can you move back into my house after all?" I propose, though I should really run this past my father.

"That's not going to happen," Trini says. "I still need to take care of Aunt Carmen while my mother looks for a job and my father works the evening shift at the warehouse. Otherwise they need to hire a nurse."

The terrible truth of the arrangement begins to sink in: Trini will be expected to continue her role as caretaker for Aunt Carmen, who hasn't recovered much after her paralyzing stroke, and Trini's father will want to make Trini his punching bag again while Trini's mother pretends nothing's going on.

"Trini, I'm so sorry," I say. "Are you girls staying for dinner? I need to get back to my station."

Lib shakes head. "No," he says. "I think this calls for a late night drive to Palm Springs. Come on, Trini. Nothing makes us feel better than yelling at old blue-haired slot machine addicts and middle-aged queens in muscle shirts."

"Hear, hear," Trini says. And they exit the restaurant more gracefully than they entered.

I take a deep breath and adjust my guayabera, but just when I thought I was in the clear for the evening, Sebastián comes back out.

"So," he says. "What's does a good-looking guy like you do for fun after hours in a one-burro town like this?"

He winks at me and my jaw drops. Never a dull moment for Mauricio Gutiérrez of Caliente Valley High.

Rendezvous

It all happens so quickly I'm not sure who proposed it first and who seconded it, but the businessmen agree it's a good idea for the teenage restaurant host to take off early and show the teenage heir of Sandoval Construction a good time while the grown-ups stay behind at Las Cazuelas and close the place down over top-shelf margaritas.

"Drive safely, Sebastián," Mr. Sandoval calls out.

"Don't you worry, Francisco," Mr. Benson says. "Maui's a good kid, right, Gutiérrez?" My father smiles nervously from his chair.

Sebastián puts his arm around my shoulder, which only elicits expressions of nostalgia from the boss about how great it is to be a young man bonding with another young man, though I suspect both our fathers know what's really up and are simply letting Mr. Benson—Mr. Menso, all right—have his moment of boys-will-be-boys for the sake of respectability.

"What a chump," Sebastián says when we get to the parking lot. "And what a *dump*. Sorry you have to work there."

I feel a bristling on the back of my neck. "It's not so bad," I say. "Las Cazuelas has seen better days, when my parents owned it."

When we get to his fancy Saab convertible it suddenly dawns on me who I'm dealing with—a guy whose pocketbook is as green and deep as his eyes. He shuts off the alarm, unlocks the doors and turns on the headlights with a one-two touch of a button on his keychain. I feel like I'm on a date on the Starship *Enterprise* and it takes every muscle in my body not to get giddy and stupid.

"Nice ride," I say. My heart pounds loudly in my chest, but I play it cool.

"Thanks, though I'm thinking of trading it in for a newer model. The cruise control is a little spotty on the freeway."

Geez. And here I am from a family that calls it a good day if no one has to pull out the jumper cables.

"Where to?" he asks.

"Well, south of here is not much," I say. "And north of here is not much with Palm Springs sticking out of it."

"North it is," Sebastián says. He folds up the roof and we speed out of the parking lot so fast I feel like I swallowed my tongue.

"You might want to ease your foot on the gas pedal," I shout. "It's a sixty-five mile an hour speed limit."

Sebastián laughs. "You're kidding?"

"Nope," I say.

"Wow," Sebastián says. "My father was right: everything runs a little slower down here. I guess this is where the punishment starts."

"What do you mean?"

Sebastián snickers. "You don't think I had a choice about moving down here with my father, did you? This is payback for getting into trouble up in Orange County. Our senior prank cost my father a pretty penny to keep my record clean, but in exchange I had to join him here in this godforsaken town—his way of making sure I don't screw up before I'm done with high school."

"So you left your friends behind?"

"A bunch of losers, anyway. I took the fall since it was my idea to set the gym on fire during the most important game of the season."

My eyes widen. "Was anyone hurt?" I ask.

"No one that matters," Sebastián says. "Just a few homo-hating jocks."

"All righty then," I say.

When we drive into the main strip in Palm Springs, I'm not surprised at how unimpressed Sebastián is by the gaudy casino lights and the parade of geriatrics strolling happily along the sidewalks because everywhere else outside of the Southwest it's cold and snowy. We end up on the downtown cruise without wanting to, which only aggravates Sebastián even more.

"Oh, brother," he says whenever other passengers shout out compliments about either the car or its gorgeous driver. He's distracted a few times with a beeping from his iPhone—his father checking up on him. He text messages a response. "Annoying," he declares as he slips the iPhone back into the case on his belt.

I'm suddenly a little ashamed about the poverty that is Caliente Valley. No, there aren't any fancy clubs for young people, except for the Boys Club, where black and Latino kids use the gym equipment for free. We've got no park or beach, except for a water park, but Sebastián doesn't seem like the type that will stand in line with his toboggan under his arm and an extra-sized towel that looks just like everybody else's extra-sized towel because everybody got theirs at the Target summer sale also. The arcade at the Lame View Mall, if it's still standing by the end of the month, will still belong to Los Calis or to any other gangs that give the young misguided men something to do in the community that won't give them jobs because there are very few to be had if you're a teenager and not a migrant farmworker. There's always Caliente Valley High, of course, institution of lesser learning, where the choices are sports, band, the drama club, or the academic decathlon—organizations so far apart from each other that they leave huge holes between them for the rest of us to fall into. So, in short, no, Sebastián Sandoval, there's nothing to do here except breathe in and breathe back out.

"Is that a gay club?" Sebastián asks as he drives into the parking lot where many other cars are also parked, the men sitting and modeling on the hoods like ornaments.

"You have to be twenty-one to get in," I say, betraying that I've been here before. In fact, the Fierce Foursome knows this parking lot all too well because this is as far as we ever got—joining the other underage lot lizards just waiting for the next cute thing to stumble out of the club, praying that he gives us some attention.

"Wow, what a motley crew. Check it out," he says.

I'm afraid to look because it suddenly dawns on me that Trini and Lib are buzzing around here like horseflies. And just when I begin to wish that they have already gone home, I hear a familiar voice:

"Hey, cupcake, how would you like my cherry on top?"

It's Trini. I sink lower into my seat.

"Oh, my God," Sebastián utters in awe. "These two are definitely the pick of the litter. We *have* to go talk to them."

"Can't we just go back to Caliente," I say in a panic. "It's getting late. My father, he worries about me, you know. And I have to be home to help my sister Mickey tidy up the place."

"Tidy up?" Sebastián says.

Next, I hear Lib's voice: "Impressive wheels. Are you guys lost? Beverly Hills is *that* way."

"Those freaks are fierce," Sebastián says. "What do they call that look? Ghetto Goth and Trailer Park Pre-Op? Is that their car or their refrigerator?"

"Can we just go?" I plead, but to no avail. Trini and Lib are too good for Sebastián to pass up, so he drives up to them.

"Maui?" the girls say in unison.

"You know these two?" Sebastián asks.

"I thought you said you worked until ten," Lib says, looking confused.

Trini walks around the car and leans on the driver's side door. "Hey, hunky," she says to Sebastián. "Ooh, green eyes! You have some Irish in you? I'd definitely like some Irish in me." She then scowls at me. "And since *when* can one order take-out at Las Cazuelas?"

"Hi, Trini. Hi, Lib," I say. "I can explain."

"Don't bother," Trini says. "I'm *so* not interested in what's happening on *that* side of the car."

Lib purses his lips. "So is this your new boyfriend? When were you planning on telling us? Were you ever going to introduce us?"

"Lib, Trini," I say. "Keep your blouses on. We just met."

Trini wraps her arms around herself, scandalized. "You're whoring?"

I roll my eyes and place my hand over my forehead. Sebastián, like a true gentleman, comes to my rescue.

"Sebastián Sandoval," he says as he extends his hand out to Trini. "I just moved into town with my father, who is currently throwing back shots of tequila with Maui's father. And since we're too young to partake, we decided to check out the scenery. And I must say: it's fabulous."

"My, my," Trini says. "You are a charmer, aren't you? We're going to get along famously. I'm Trinidad Ramos: diva, dangerous and delicious. But you can call me Trini. And my partner in sin over there is Liberace García—Lib. Don't let the vampire outfit fool you. She don't bite—she only nibbles." Trini pantomimes the nibbling into the air.

"Pleasure to meet you," Sebastián says as he extends his arm through the open window to shake hands with Lib.

"*Enchanté,*" Lib replies.

"Silly faggot," Trini says. "French is for flamers."

I jump in: "Anyway, we were on our way back to the restaurant, if you don't mind. I have a feeling I'm going to be driving my father home tonight."

"Yes," Sebastián says. "But we will meet again, Trini, Lib. Since I'll be completing my senior year with all of you at Caliente Valley High."

Trini applauds. "How ab-fabby is that? We can be the Fierce Foursome all over again. Of course, there is the minor matter of the initiation."

"Initiation?" Lib says.

"Don't you remember?" Trini says, winking at Lib. "Pledging members have to sleep with *all* of the founding members. I'll sacrifice myself and go first."

Lib gives Trini the stare down, I shake my head. "Let's just go, Sebastián," I say. "It's getting out of control. We'll see you girls at the Queer Planter, first thing Monday morning."

"Actually," Trini says. "I was hoping you and Lib could come over this weekend and help me move things around the house? I have permanent guests, remember?"

I remember: Mr. and Mrs. Ramos. The unhappy family back together again.

"Call me," I say. "See you later, Lib."

As Lib waves and Trini blows kisses, Sebastián and I head out of Palm Springs, and back on the I-10 to get to Caliente. I can't help but slide back into the memory of Isaac and our drives through the town at night, when the voices of the people go quiet, the faces of the population become invisible, and all that's left is the non-judgmental landscape of lights, our safety secure inside the cocoon of the car. I miss him, suddenly, and not even this gorgeous man behind the wheel can take his place.

"Colorful duo, especially the one in polka-dots," Sebastián finally says.

"Sorry about that," I say. "But you'll get used to it. Under all that costume are two of the most wonderful people you'll ever know. It's tough to be different here in the Caliente Valley."

"It's tough to be different anywhere," Sebastián says. "Though I can see how it's particularly challenging in a place that lacks class and sophistication."

That bristling on the back of my neck again. This time I don't stay silent.

"You know," I say. "I know this isn't Orange County and no one you met so far drives a fancy car and carries an iPhone, but this is where I live—we're poor here, but we're also proud. I'd really appreciate it if you slipped your attitude back into its leather case and kept it stored while you're hanging around me and my friends. That's assuming you're going to want to be seen with us, I mean, there are a few kids at the high school who can probably relate to your lifestyle a little better than we can, and you can go skiing up in Big Bear or attend concerts in Anaheim or sip virgin daiquiris at Redondo Beach, or I don't know what else you people with cash to burn do with your time while the rest of us keep it real with our low-wage jobs at the local Mexican restaurant where, believe it or not, some people live for the Taco Tuesday happy hour. But if you're okay with that, then I'll be okay with you, and we can—"

I stop as soon as the car begins to pull over to the shoulder. "What are you doing?"

Sebastián turns off the ignition.

"You're not going to kick me out of the car, are you?"

The he grabs the back of my head with one hand and presses my face into his.

How to describe that kiss? Maybe I can begin there, with the word. It isn't a kiss. This is Latino-on-Latino action, so it's more like a *beso!* Exclamation mark at the end. It's that spinning wheel at the top of a fireworks castle lit up to celebrate the patron saint of every Mexican village. It's the first bite into the sweetbread compressed with the final bite into the sweetbread and then rolled around and around in the mouth. It's the two stocky bodies in a *lucha libre* match colliding at the center of a wrestling ring and surrounded by throngs of whistling. It's the letters of *Sebastián* reshuffled into the letters of *Mauricio* and then fanned out into a lovely guttural implosion of syllables, like the word *murcielago*, in which every vowel of the alphabet gets to rise and sing. And then there's that lump in my pants, but that isn't anything special. I'm a teenager. I get one of those like once an hour.

When he finally unlocks his mouth from mine, Sebastián looks at me—no, he penetrates me with the emerald arrows of his eyes and asks, "Do you want to have sex?"

I let out the most unsexy sound in my vocabulary: "Uhhh..."

"I know," Sebastián says as he leans back on his seat. "This isn't even a date. Damn, I'm moving too fast. Sorry, Maui. You deserve better."

"Yeah," I say, relieved that I don't have to explain more, like that I'm actually saving it for the right occasion and for the right guy, even though just a few minutes ago a late-night drive on the I-10 with the son of a construction magnate seemed just about right to me.

"I mean, just because you're poor doesn't mean you're cheap," Sebastián adds.

I suck my teeth. "What? Look, just take me back Las Cazuelas, I have to drive my father home."

"What did I say?" Sebastián asks, earnestly. And that's why it pisses me off, because he doesn't know an insult even if it's a nettle tumbling off his tongue.

We drive back to the parking lot in silence, though this time Sebastián fills the void by playing Lady Gaga. I'm in love with Judas, all right.

The man-bonding at Las Cazuelas appears to have gone a little better. Mr. Sandoval slaps Mr. Benson on the back and my father looks much more relaxed than when we left.

"Don't be careless, Benson, let us give you a ride home," Mr. Sandoval pleads. "Gutiérrez here has his boy to take care of him. How was the joyride, fellas?"

"Educational," Sebastián says. And for no apparent reason the three men burst out laughing. "Oh, brother," Sebastián adds under his breath.

In the end, Mr. Benson climbs in the back seat of the Saab and sets off with the best-looking father and son pair that Caliente Valley will ever see. Sebastián can barely muster a "See you in class, Maui."

I take the keys to my father's beat-up old Cadillac and I suddenly realize what it's like to be demoted. But I'd rather be in this car than in Sebastián's schmancy Saab at the moment, that's for certain.

"How did it go?" Papi asks.

"You stink," I say and pinch my nose to keep out the smell of cigarettes and stale tequila breath.

"Sorry," Papi says. "Occasions like these don't come around that often, but you know I have to do it. The boss."

"I know," I say. "Open the window at least. Get some fresh air."

I turn the ignition, the clunker gets started and we get going, but we're barely out of the lot when Papi starts to pry.

"So, Sebastián seems like a nice kid."

"He burned down the gym at his old school," I fire back.

And before he has a chance to ask his next question I add: "With people in it."

"Oh," he says. "Crap."

After a few intersections, Papi feels inspired to ask another question. "He didn't suggest anything inappropriate, right?"

My body stiffens. But then I think: this is my father, he deserves to know the truth. "No, Papi, I didn't have sex with him, though we both wanted to when he pulled the car over to the side of the road. We just locked lips a little, you know, made out."

I turn to look at my father and he looks pale, sober suddenly.

"I was actually referring to drugs or alcohol," he says. "You know, these rich kids think they can get away with anything. But, I'm glad nothing else happened either, now that you mention it."

I'm mortified. But then my father and I look at each other and burst into laughter. That keeps us awake until we get home and find Mickey sitting on the couch with a towel turban on her head. Papi and I stumble in, embracing each other.

"Papi, have you been drinking?" Mickey says, shaking her head. "Nice role modeling for Maui."

"Just tonight, sweetheart," he says. He walks to his room on his own.

I sit down next to Mickey and let out a deep sigh.

"What's the matter with you?" she asks. She doesn't take her eyes off the television.

"I think I'm about to enter into my first love-hate relationship," I say.

Mickey turns to me and then flings her arms around me. "Oh, honey," she says. "You're growing up!"

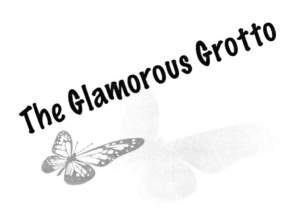

The Glamorous Grotto

On Saturday afternoon, Mr. García drops Lib off at my house, and then Mickey drops us off at Trini's. All is well, all is perfectly normal until the front door opens and standing before us is an unrecognizable, rather plain-looking *dude*, who looks somewhat familiar. Lib and I are speechless.

"Trini?" I venture to guess.

"Hi," Trini says through her pout.

"What on God's transsexual earth happened to you?" Lib says. "You look like a plucked chicken."

"Lib!" I say. "A little more sensitivity, please."

"Lib's right," Trini says. "The only way I could be uglier is if the color of my belt didn't match the color of my shoes."

I step forward to give her—him—her—this is going to get tricky from now on—a hug. "Oh, darling, Trini," I say. "This must feel horrible. Boy pants, boy shirt, no eyeliner. I hope you're at least wearing your pink Saturday panties."

"It doesn't matter. This whole outfit feels like it's made of poison oak. I'm itching all over." She scratches for full effect.

"Well, let's go in and maybe put a nice lady hat on your head," I say. "That should take the edge off."

"How's Aunt Carmen doing?" Lib asks, craning his neck to check.

I walk Trini to the couch and we sit next to each other.

"Aunt Carmen's sleeping," Trini says. "That's all she can do nowadays, poor thing. I still play her old records in the afternoons, which puts a nice smile on her face, but other than that there's no other evidence that she's still breathing."

"All righty then," I say.

"And what about this—drag?" Lib says, pointing at Trini's clothes. "It's your father's doing, isn't it?"

Trini nods her head and says, "It's one of the concessions I have to make before they move in here tomorrow, though they're coming in this afternoon to check that I cleared out enough space for their things. We all have to downsize, which sucks because that spare bedroom is my walk-in closet."

I take a deep breath and look around at the old lady museum around me as I say, "I just can't imagine Aunt Carmen's not being Aunt Carmen's. You know what I mean?"

"Yeah," Lib agrees. "Walking in here is like walking into a Latin American theater. The floors don't creak, they mambo."

"So the plan is this, girls," Trini says, picking up the excitement in her voice. "I'm converting the shed in the back into my walk-in-slash-hang-out-in closet, which my father didn't object to, believe you me. It'll be like a miniature version of what we're sitting in now, which needs to go since my mother has to bring in all her crap, including that recliner my father plops himself in after work. We'll move as much as we can from the living room into Aunt Carmen's bedroom, just enough to allow a person to walk in and out with the bedpan, except that the faux Tiffany lamps, the velvet divan, and the glass coffee table with hand-carved legs stay—they go to the shed, which henceforth shall be known as: *The Glamorous Grotto*."

"Are your eyes rolling as far back into your head as they are in mine?" Lib says to me.

"Lib!" I say. "We're here to help, so let's help."

"Thank you, Maui," Trini says. "Okay, chop-chop. Put your back into it, boys, and don't scratch the coffee table—it's vintage."

"And what are *you* going to do, Princess Pucker-up?" Lib asks.

"Supervise, of course," Trini says, throwing her hands into the air. "To the task at hand, grunts!"

"Trini!" I complain.

"All right," she says, "I'm just pulling the Goth kid's leg, for crying out loud. Here, you grab that end of the divan, Midnight Lips. And be careful!"

After much huffing and puffing, we manage to set up the somewhat cramped, but in a cozy kind of way, Glamorous Grotto in the back shed. On the plus side, Trini can spend her time here and drag out into the night without shocking the hell out of her parents, but she'll need to switch back into her boy duds if she wants to go in and use the loo. It's comfy, it's quaint, and definitely queer, but no matter how one looks at it, this is nothing short of being forced back into the closet—literally.

"I like it," Trini says when she sits back on the divan, her legs crossed. "It's dramatic, flamboyant, and fierce! I probably won't need a bedroom at Aunt Carmen's at all."

"I kind of like it, too," I admit. "Maybe this can be our own private Mariposa Club hideaway."

Lib's eyebrows shoot up. "Hey, you're right!" he says. "We can plot the queer takeover of Caliente Valley High from here!"

"Hold on to your torpedoes, Comrade García," Trini says. "School hasn't even started yet. Plus, you forget the other thing we talk about at the Mariposa Club: boys." Trini turns to me. "So, girlfriend: dish."

I redden. "There's really nothing to tell," I say. "Sebastián's a nice guy, but a little complicated."

Lib cocks an eye. "Oh? How so?"

"Well," I say. "Maybe you should come to your own conclusions when you meet him. That is if he's even going to hang out with us. He might not. But then again, he might."

"He's too good for us, isn't he?" Lib says. "I knew it. I had him pegged from the moment he drove up in his schmancy car. A Saab convertible, no less. Do you realize that car costs more than my family's house?"

"How embarrassing," Trini says. "He must have laughed at my Paulina Rubio."

"He called it a refrigerator," I say.

Trini gasps. "If Paulina Rubio were to be called a household appliance, she'd be no less than an espresso machine." Trini makes the sound of steam escaping: *ssssssss!*

"Well, I'm not sure he's Fierce Foursome material," Lib says. "I mean, we're members of the Mariposa Club, we're activists and socialists. And feminists, I think."

"And economists," Trini adds. "I mean, we're operating the organization on a shoe-string budget."

Lib looks askance at Trini. "Yeah. Right. Anyway, sorry, Maui, but your Rockefeller is a Rottenfella and we have no place for a poison weed at the Queer Planter."

"Geez, Lib," I say. "Strain your metaphors, much? I can't believe you two. I mean, you barely even met him and already you're making these grand pronouncements against him just because he comes from money and we don't. I'll admit, he grated on me a few times, but he just arrived. He has to adjust, and learn, and grow. He's as much of an outsider as any one of us. Everyone has a right to reinvent himself—you of all people should know about that."

"Then just answer me this," Lib says. "Do you like him?"

I keep quiet for a second longer than I had intended to.

"I see," Lib says.

"See what, Lib?" I say.

Trini chimes in: "Yeah, Lib. See what?"

Lib shakes his head. "Don't you get it, Trini? Maui's got the hots for the rich boy, so now he's going to make us compromise our integrity just so he can have his eye candy join the club. It's Yoko Ono all over again."

"Yoko Ono?" I say. "What are you talking about?"

Trini looks dazed. "I have to confess, Lib, I'm not on the same planet you're on at the moment either."

"That's because you don't read and you put too many chemicals on your head."

"That's not true," Trini says. "I've read every issue of *People Magazine* at Von's Market and I haven't home-permed my hair since last summer."

"Why do I even try?" Lib says with exasperation.

"Look," I say. "I'm not asking that we make him club president or anything, I'm just saying we test him out. We're going to plan something big, aren't we? So let's see what kinds of ideas he can bring to the table. Let's invite him. There's nothing more energizing to a group than fresh blood."

"Not to mention fresh meat," Trini says.

I put my hand on Trini's shoulder. "Sweetheart, you're not helping."

"Okay, I'll stay out of it. Call me Marie Antoinette and cut my head off, why don't you?"

"Well, I'm a member of this club also and I have every right to object to a proposal, don't I?" Lib says.

I sigh. "You want due process, bring it! I say we take a vote, then. All in favor of inviting Sebastián Sandoval to be part of the Mariposa Club say aye. Aye!"

Lib follows suit: "All opposed say nay. Nay!"

Lib and I both look down at Trini.

"What?" Trini says. "Oh, so now I have to speak up, don't I? Well, well, well, fortunes reverse quicker here than in a Mexican telenovela. Let me see if I got this right." She gets up and paces back and forth between Lib and me. "If I say *Aye*, we get to hang out with the best slice of pie to arrive to this crusty oven we call Caliente Valley. It will definitely score us some points with the popular crowd, not to mention that a generous financial contribution from his piggy bank might let us dream flashier and glitzier. And if I say *Nay* it will be business as usual with limited ambitions and a shrinking membership now that Isaac is gone and Maddy is preggers and probably more preoccupied with her health than with our fabulousness. What to do? What to do?"

"Think with your brains and not with your bra straps," Lib says.

I go for the cheap shot: "Have you ever ridden in a Saab convertible?"

"Aye!" Trini says.

"Motion passes, two to one," I declare.

Lib remains tight-lipped.

"Meeting adjourned," I say.

"He gets one chance," Lib whispers slowly.

Before I have time to object to that, we hear Mrs. Ramos call out from the house: "Trinidad, are you out there?"

Trini pulls out of the group and exits the Glamorous Grotto. "We're back here, Mama. We're done putting the extra furniture into storage."

Lib and I don't even have time to finish our stare down, but we exit the Grotto knowing full well we have left some business unfinished.

"Hello, Mrs. Ramos," we say. "Hello, Mr. Ramos."

"You boys did a wonderful job," Mrs. Ramos says. "Didn't they, Mr. Ramos?"

Mr. Ramos, looking displeased and constipated, doesn't even crack a smile. And for another few seconds, neither will I.

Sunday Brunch

Though there's a broad spectrum to the kinds of customers who show up at Las Cazuelas for weekend brunch, most of these fall into two opposing categories: the church-goers and the drunks. The church-goers come in looking sharp in their Sunday best—girls and ladies in conservative dresses, men wearing ties or at the very least sporting a nicely-pressed guayabera in a shade of brown or blue. They leave their Bibles in the car but pray at the table and they smile excessively. They patronize the buffet. The drunks look scruffy and sleepy, they come in wearing flea market t-shirts or unfashionable sweat suits and tennis shoes, though they haven't set foot in the gym since the last millennium, and they come in for the *menudo*—Mexico's premier hangover medicine—spicy red stew of hominy and cow stomach. The only thing they have in common is that neither group knows how to tip—that's the word according to the gospel of Yolanda.

"Brunch is really like a service to the Mexican housewife," Yolanda tells me. "It's the one day of the week she doesn't have to cook." She stops one of the servers and lowers her voice: "Make sure you save a bowl of *menudo* for me in the back. We ran out last week." The server nods his head and moves on.

"Anyway," Yolanda continues, "There's very little energy left to complain or to make unreasonable demands while they stuff their faces for an hour, even if they douse themselves in *café con leche*. So Sunday brunch is as slow and boring as their metabolisms. Bring a book next time, kid."

"Gotcha," I say.

Since Yolanda's the expert, she's right. Nothing exciting happens while people roll in and then roll back out of Las Cazuelas. The ones doing all the blood-pumping are the busboys, the servers and the hosts—all of us maneuvering around each other as we keep the cycle of bodies turning like a wooden spoon in a thick pot of *mole poblano*. Only occasionally is there something worth really noticing, like when Maddy and Snake walk in through the door, still looking like they're high on wedded bliss. They both keep putting their hands on her belly though Maddy's just beginning to show her pregnancy.

"Hey!" I say. "Long time no see, guys."

"Hi, Mauricio," Maddy leans forward to give me a kiss on the cheek, which makes me blush. "How's Mickey? I haven't seen her in a while either."

"She's fine. Ready to transfer up to UC Riverside in the fall," I say.

"Well, give her our best," Snake says.

"Table for two?" I ask.

"Actually, three," Maddy says, rubbing her belly. Snakes lets out a chuckle and leans over to kiss her. If it weren't Maddy and Snake, I'd say *ugh!*

I take them to a table and give them the spiel: "Your server will be right with you." I'm about to walk away when I decide to throw in a personal connection: "And I guess I'll see you in class tomorrow, guys."

Maddy's face changes, which makes me pause. "Actually, Maui, Walter and I are finishing up our high school degrees through the Independent Study Program."

Snake chimes in: "Yeah, we both got jobs with the Sandoval Construction project. I'm building and Maddy's filing. Gotta save money for the kid, you know."

"Oh," I say. "Well, I'll miss you guys. I'll see you around, then."

"Bye," Maddy says, waving her fingers.

I walk back to my station feeling as if this moment signals the beginning of a wave of *bye-bye, see you later, and have a good life.* But before I can dwell on it any further, here come the Garcías, Celie towering above all of them in her funereal gown.

"Mauricio!" Mr. García says, wrapping his arm around my torso to give me a hug.

Mrs. García smiles. "How's your papa?" she asks.

"Good," I answer. "It's been fun working here together, but we really don't cross paths much. He's always holed up in his office."

"Running a restaurant is hard work," Mr. García replies. I nod politely.

"Hey, champ," Celie says, giving me a punch on the shoulder. "Heard you and Lib are having a family feud. Take care of it, will you? He's driving me nuts."

"Celie!" Lib says. He's been hiding behind her the entire time.

"Hey," I say to Lib.

"Hey," he says back to me.

"Well, that's a start," Celie says.

"I'll take you to your table." I guide the Garcías to the larger dining area. It's closer to the buffet table and the overpowering smell of cheese makes my mouth water. "Your server will be right with you," I say.

"Great, because we're celebrating today," Celie says. She rubs her hands together.

"It's not your birthday, is it?" I ask.

Mr. García shakes his head proudly. "Celie's got a new job running security for Sandoval Construction."

"Yeah," Celie says. "Since the Plane View Mall is shutting down soon, I had to bail before I was out of a paycheck."

"Congrats," I say.

"Thanks," Celie says.

"And thank you, Mauricio," Mrs. García says.

"See you tomorrow, Lib," I add in a flat tone.

"See you tomorrow, Maui," Lib responds, matching that flat tone.

By the time I reach my station, Yolanda's back from her cigarette break.

"Getting the hang of it?" she asks.

"Piece of *tres leches* cake. Hey, this Sandoval Construction thing is for real, isn't it?"

Yolanda nods her head. "It sure is. Everyone I know either got a job there already or knows someone who did."

"Same here," I say.

I step back a little to take in the whole picture: the arrival of the Sandovals isn't about me, it's about the community, about saving people from economic heartache. Our center, the mall, lame as it stands, is still our center, and it's about to collapse and put even more people out of work. But deep down inside I feel a little resentful that the powerful will become more powerful still, and that Sebastián will be a force to be reckoned with, if only by association. He came on strong last night, and shoved his tongue into my mouth with the confidence of a guy who gets everything he wants. And I need to sort out why I'm drawn to him: is it the wealth and privilege or is it the type of chemistry that transcends class and upbringing? I guess I'll find out.

Yolanda taps me on the shoulder. "Uh-oh. The principal's coming."

I look up. Papi—I mean—Mr. Gutiérrez is swiftly making his way toward us.

"Good morning, Mr. Gutiérrez," Yolanda and I say at once.

"Good morning, good morning," my father says. "Maui, can I speak with you for a minute? Come with me."

I shrug at Yolanda and follow my father into the side room where a few of the workers are dismantling the Three Kings Day set.

"Something wrong, Mr. Gutiérrez?" I say.

My father shakes his head. "No, nothing at all. I just got off the phone with Mr. Benson and we're planning ahead a little bit. Remember I told you about the Mexican curio market we're setting up in here?"

The room could definitely work out. I can see it now: a wall of Day of the Dead figurines, a few miniature piñatas, Mexican blankets, maybe some pottery. And of course, an array of t-shirts and aprons with the Las Cazuelas logo on it. Tacky and trinket cheap, but with penny profits with every purchase that should not be scoffed at during the recession.

"Well," I say. "It will definitely give your patrons something to do while they're waiting for their table on busy nights. When do you plan to open?"

My father scratches his head. "We're thinking maybe in a month, once all the merchandise comes in from Mexico City. We can connect it to our February second event."

"Groundhog Day?" I ask.

"Well, Candlemas," my father corrects me. "*Día de la Candelaria*, south of the border. We'll have to make sure we've got plenty of dolls."

"Sounds good," I say.

"Yes," my father says, "it is good. It'll give the restaurant a new feature, keeping us fresh. It'll bring in some extra funds and give me a chance to create another job or two. That's why I wanted to talk to you. The offer still stands if you want to work in the curio market instead of hosting."

"Sales, huh?" I wonder out loud, which my father misinterprets as hesitation.

"You would be trained, of course," my father says. "The market will only open in the afternoons and into the evenings, when there's more traffic coming through the restaurant. What do you say?"

I weigh my options: hosting usually means more face-to-face interaction, like I had at Joyería Dutton, though if I do sales, that's also familiar territory. I'll have to stand with both jobs, but hosting is all about the people, and selling is all about the goods. Hosting, selling, hosting, selling...and then it hits me. *Brilliant!*

"When do I have to give you an answer?" I ask.

My father shrugs his shoulder. "It'll be nice to let Mr. Benson know sooner than later."

"Let me think about it for a few more minutes and get back to you, Mr. Gutiérrez," I say. "And if I can't do it, might I suggest someone who can?"

"I don't see why not. Okay, well, let me know." He takes off to his office.

As soon as my father's gone I rush past the hostess counter, weave through the bodies of servers, busboys and customers, and stop at the Garcías' table.

"You're back," Celie says. "Just in time for some flan."

"No, thank you," I say. "I actually came to ask Lib something important."

Lib looks up at me surprised. "Oh? And it can't wait until our first club meeting tomorrow at school?"

"Libbie," Celie says. "Don't be an ass—terisk."

"Mauricio has been nothing but gracious to us since we arrived, mijo," Mr. García says. "You can extend him the same courtesy."

Lib lowers his head, and then raises it again. "I'm sorry, Maui. And I'm sorry, also, family."

"That's better," Mrs. García says. "Go ahead, Maui. What do you need to ask Lib? Or is it personal?"

I take a deep breath. "I wanted to ask Lib if he'd be interested in working at the new Mexican curio market that's going to be opening here in the restaurant next month. You did mention, didn't you, Lib, that you were looking for an after-school job? How perfect would this one be? We could both just walk over here after classes."

"That sounds like da bomb, Lib," Celie says. "It would certainly relieve some pressure off mom's purse. Not to mention mine."

"It would be nice for you to have some pocket money once you head out to college," Mr. García adds.

Lib looks flabbergasted, which he should. I mean, here I am offering him employment, not just anywhere but within spitting distance of me, and there he is giving me the shark eye from the moment he set foot in the restaurant. I'd feel like beef jerky, too!

"I don't know what to say," Lib says. "Except, it would be great. Where can I put in my application?"

"Just right over there at the manager's office," I say. "I think it would work out best if we both went in to talk to my father together. That is, if you have your father's permission."

"Permission granted," Mr. García blurts out. "Go, go!"

The excitement of the moment is enough for us to be friends again, at least for the time being. We almost skip over to my father's office like schoolgirls since this is probably one of the best ideas I've had of late. I can't imagine how this can go wrong. And besides, a small part of me is glad that good old Las Cazuelas, Caliente Valley's own homegrown Mexican eatery, can still do something Sandoval Construction takes for granted: offer one of the local citizens a job. But before I knock on my father's office door, I pause: who am I really doing this for? For Lib? For myself? For peace with my friend or for war with the huge conglomerate that's poised to take over our community? I knock three times. For now, it doesn't really matter.

Rigoberto González

Mariposa Resurrection

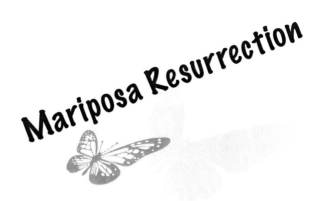

Trini is unfashionably late to the Queer Planter. I mean, she always makes a grand entrance but this time she comes dressed as a boy. Since this is the first day of school after winter break, I expected she would show up in something fluffy, not flannel. Lib and I look at each other in disbelief.

"Oh. My. Goddess. Not again," Lib says. "If she keeps this up she's going to be stripped of her tiara."

I shush him: "Don't make such a big stink about it. It must be killing her inside."

"Wassup, boys?" Trini says through a thick voice.

"Trini, stop that," I say. "You're scaring the children."

Trini relaxes into a more familiar and feminine pose. "Tell me about it. I scared myself in the rear view mirror. I almost ran Paulina Rubio off the road. Who would've thought I'd have to walk around again in my prison uniform? But next time I'm going to be smarter and leave an outfit in the trunk, maybe change between periods or something."

"I guess that could work," Lib says. He then reaches over to turn Trini's head. "Hey, what the hell is this?"

Trini covers a bruise with the palm of her hand. "Oh," she says. "Nothing painful, just a goodbye kiss from daddy."

My jaw drops. Not this again! "Trini, he can't lay a finger on you like that."

"Oh, believe me," Trini fires back, all cocky. "It wasn't a finger."

"You know what I mean!" I say. "There are laws against this kind of thing. You could have him arrested, even."

Trini's mood shifts to angry. "Look, you two. Don't even breathe a word about this to anyone! I'll take care of this, all right. But mind your own damn business. My family can't afford these kinds of problems right now."

"But it's your father who's creating them," Lib chimes in.

"I said, zip it! It's not really about me, you know, it's about the hard times we're going through. He just doesn't know how to deal with it, that's all."

No one dares to speak for the next minute and we simply stand there locked in thought. I know *my* head is buzzing. Yet another dilemma to contend with: to open my mouth and get my friend's father into trouble, or to keep silent and allow the abuse against my friend to continue. It just doesn't seem right. Trini has suffered enough already. Thankfully, the arrival of our new member gives us something else to focus on.

"Hey, guys," Sebastián says. "Sorry I'm late. I had to find a good parking spot. My father's afraid my car's going to get stolen or vandalized, so I had to argue with him about letting me drive to school."

Lib and I give each other a knowing look: oh, what we would give to have those kinds of oppressions.

"The car will be fine, Sebastián," I say. "You remember Lib. And Trini."

Sebastián raises an eyebrow when he looks at Trini. "Did you do something different to your hair?" he asks.

Trini grins. "Hi, handsome. My, you're like a tall glass of water when you're not sitting in your chariot. Sorry you have to see me like this. I usually have much better fashion sense, but today was one of those days when I looked into the closet and said, 'No, none of this will do!' So in a fit of desperation I ran out into the street and took the first outfit I saw. Unfortunately, it was the Mexican leaf blower's."

Sebastián chuckles. "You're a funny one, aren't you?"

And just like that, the first bell rings and we have to postpone our meeting until lunch, which doesn't bother me in the least this time. It's going to be one of those days, all right.

Now that Lib has become a senior officially, his schedule has been adjusted over the break and it matches mine exactly, so we start out the morning in chemistry. There, we compare notes with Sebastián, whose schedule also matches ours, except that unlike the rest of the Mariposa Club, he has chosen *not* to opt out of physical education during third period. Suddenly, my chest flushes at the thought of Sebastián walking around the boys locker room in the buff.

"That's too bad," Lib whispers. "Because we hang out at the library and call it study hour. It's actually fun."

We're keeping our voices down since we're not paying attention to the morning announcements coming through as static through the intercom or to the new chemistry teacher, What's-his-name. Ever since our beloved Ms. McAllister was retired because of her bad health, many of us have lost interest in science.

And no one has yet knocked his head and become interested in second period English with Mr. Knowles, or Mr. Doze, rather. But seizing on the novelty of a new student present, Dozey makes a big production out of introducing Sebastián to the class.

"And tell us, Mr. Sandoval," Mr. Knowles says. "What was the last book you read?"

Sebastián pulls out a thick text from his backpack. "I'm actually right in the middle of this one, sir," he responds. That "sir" definitely scores him points. "*The Red and the Black* by Stendhal."

Dozey's impressed. "Marvelous!" he says. I roll my eyes. "And what is Monsieur Julien Sorel up to at the moment?"

"Julien has just escaped the lovesick clutches of Mme de Rênal and fled to the seminary in Bensançon."

Mr. Doze titters in delight at Sebastián's pronunciation of those French names. Lib looks at me horrified: a kid showing interest in high school English? He's going to get his ass kicked.

"Take note, students," Mr. Knowles announces, pointing at Sebastián. "This young man will go very far." Eye daggers begin to fly from all directions.

Sebastián takes the compliment in stride, as if he's used to this kind of flattery. As if he's entitled to it. The rest of the period drags on without mercy, and there's no other reaction made in class until Mr. Knowles holds up a copy of this semester's reading: *East of Eden* by John Steinbeck. The girth of the book alone elicits a general groan, except from Sebastián, whose *The Red and the Black* is just as thick.

Between periods, as Sebastián heads to the gym and Lib and I head to the library for study hour, I decide to give our new mariposa a tip.

"I consider myself a bookworm also. But I don't wave that around. It just brings out all kinds of negative energy," I tell him, knowing full well that I'm being a hypocrite because just last year Lib was showing off his smarts as well. Not a word out of Lib, either, who walks one step behind me.

Sebastián stops. We almost collide into him. "I don't apologize for anything. Not for my wealth, not for academic diligence. I leave that kind of cowardice to the weak," he says. My face grows warm.

"Which way to the gym?" he asks. Lib points to the right and Sebastián walks away.

I'm still trying to cool off fifteen minutes later as Lib and I are sitting across the table from Trini. Mr. Gump sits at the check-out counter, reading *The New York Times*.

"Well, I never," Trini says after we tell her about our exchange with Sebastián. "But you know, Maui, he's right."

Lib and I give Trini our furious mariposa scowls.

"Don't look at me like that," Trini says. "Think about it: he didn't call you weak. He said not being *yourself* is a sign of weakness. That's two different things."

"Says she who's now walking around looking like Paul Bunyan?" Lib interjects.

Trini turns her head up. "That's different," she says. "I'm being *forced* to dress this way. And believe you me as soon as I turn eighteen and move out of the house, I'm burning this whack potato sack."

"Shh!" Mr. Gump warns us.

"Good morning, Mr. Gump!" Trini yells back. "How are you doing today! Anything interesting in the paper?"

Mr. Gump simply glares at Trini. He has long ago ceased trying to battle with her, so he turns the newspaper page and hides behind it.

"Anywho," Trini continues, giving Mr. Gump the hand. "You're being a pair of big meanies to little ol' Sebastián Sandoval, well read *and* probably well hung. Sounds to me like the true green-eyed monsters are here, sitting right in front of me."

My mouth goes dry. Trini's absolutely right. I'm jealous. And confused about my crush on Sebastián. There are so many reasons to like him and just as many to dislike him. Part of me wants to surrender. The other part to conquer—and not in a romantic sense. Suddenly I remember my advice to Lib and Trini at the Glamorous Grotto: *Give Sebastián a chance. Don't judge him so quickly.* Maybe I should practice what I preach.

I sigh. "Well, we'll have our meeting at lunch. I told Sebastián we hold court at the Queer Planter. And let's try to steer clear of personality conflicts, girls, and focus. Before we know it this year's going to be over and if we don't do something to leave our footprint on these grounds no one will ever know we walked here. Agreed?"

"Agreed," Lib says.

"Hell to the yes," Trini says. "Oh, and by the way, I hope you all caught the announcement during first period: next week every senior club has to report to the gym during senior break for the yearbook photographs. So look dazzling."

We hold off on any further discussion and spend the rest of study hour catching Trini up on our employment opportunities. Though she feels a bit left out, we all know that her function is as Aunt Carmen's caretaker in the afternoons. She keeps saying, *But don't worry, I'll be free soon,* as if the end of high school is also the end of some jail sentence. I don't quite understand it. In June, once we all graduate, Aunt Carmen will still be bed-bound, Trini will still be living with her parents, and, based on how Mr. Ramos is able to control Trini's wardrobe so severely, it's also doubtful that he'll loosen up about that within the next six months. Unless Trini plans on running away. Just like Isaac ran away. The thought brings a pang of hurt to my chest and I lower my head.

"You okay, Maui?" Lib asks, placing his hand on my shoulder. I nod. It's lunch time.

Since we can't afford to go off campus for lunch, we head for a quick pick-up at the cafeteria, which is crowded and noisy and smells like the counters have been polished with the oil bubbling for the potato fries. Only Lib and Trini qualify for a free meal. I have to pay a dollar, which isn't asking much for a fish sandwich, a soda, an apple and a bag of chips. I'd like to say we went in and out, but the process is actually painfully burdensome since students at Caliente Valley High don't know how to talk and move the line at the same time.

"Beep beep!" Trini calls out. "Can the fat person at the front please shift to drive?"

The fat person Trini has just aggravated turns around and flips Trini the bird.

"I'm sorry," Trini says. "No habla español."

I shake my head.

"What happened to your blouse, faggot?" One of the popular blonde girls in line just behind us looks at Trini in shock.

Trini doesn't miss a beat. "Same thing that's going to happen to your face by the age of twenty, white girl: wrinkles. Stay out of the sun."

On impulse, the blonde girl touches her face in a panic, and then realizes she's been had when those around her start to laugh. She rolls her eyes and keeps to herself for the rest of the time we're in line.

Back at the Queer Planter, Sebastián has his little fancy canisters spread out in front of him.

"Did he bring his cat food?" Lib whispers under his breath.

"Keep it friendly, Lib," I remind him, though that is what the canisters look like—cans of pet food.

"Are you on one of those macrobiotic diet fads?" Trini asks.

Sebastián smiles. "Our housekeeper prepares lunch for both my father and me," he says. "Fast food is not very healthy."

I hesitate pulling out my greasy fish hiding inside a two-inch thick slab of butter-grilled bread. Instead, I bite into my apple.

Sebastián uses chopsticks to eat, not his fingers like the rest of us. He's got spinach dumplings in one canister, fresh tofu in another, and some sort of mango concoction he calls chutney in the third little tin container.

"I'll trade you a few chips for a dumpling," Trini dares to offer, and it makes me angry somehow. Or maybe the feeling is shame.

"Uhm," Sebastián says. "Sure." When he smiles as Trini makes a dive for the dumpling I want to slap them both: Trini for acting like such a deprived poor person and Sebastián for the display of condescension.

Lib looks at the second dumpling with a bit of longing, and when Sebastián offers it to him I'm expecting Lib to speak up on our behalf, to be proud enough to refuse it and righteous enough to call him on this small gesture of pity disguised as generosity. I can already hear the opening of the reprimand: *Why don't you keep your soggy dumpling and choke on it!*

But instead, I'm floored when Lib takes it with glee and says, "Thanks!"

Am I missing something? Did this just happen in front of me? I exhale deeply.

"What?" Lib says through his mouthful of dumpling.

"So let's not waste any more time, girls," I say. "I call the meeting to order."

Since this is Sebastián's first meeting we clarify our brief but eventful organizational history, how we began as an LGBT club, then became, under the leadership of Liberace García, a Gay/Straight Alliance, which didn't fare any better than its previous manifestation, so we're regrouping to re-envision and re-direct our efforts in order to fulfill our fuzzy mission: to do right by the Caliente Valley High queers, past, present and future.

"I'd like to propose we have a gay prom," Trini blurts out.

Lib twists his lip, and then says, "Not to pooh-pooh your prom, Trini, but do we even have enough out queers in this school to hold such an event? I mean, with the four of us we might be able to hold a gay square dance."

"Let's hear her out, Lib," I say. "Would you like to elaborate, Trini?"

"Certainly," Trini says. "I'd like to propose we have a gay prom and that Sebastián propose to me."

"Good grief," Lib says.

I purse my lips. "All righty, then. Any other ideas?"

Lib raises his hand to speak. "I'd like to propose," he says. "That we challenge the debate team in a public forum on the issue of gay marriage, gay adoption, and citizenship for gay international couples."

"Oh, we will surely sell tickets to that event," Trini says, doing her pretend yawn. "We should think ahead about how to keep the scalpers at bay."

"Can you think about anything else besides parties?" Lib asks Trini.

"And can you think about anything else besides politics?" Trini fires back.

I step in. "Girls, relax, this is a brainstorming session. Let's just bounce some ideas back and forth without getting all defensive. Now, I think both of these proposals have potential, but let's be realistic. Unless we involve at least four other high schools, I'm not sure we're going to achieve the gay prom body count. Something like this takes a lot more planning than just a few months before the big night. And the whole gay debate sounds overwhelming and, frankly, I'm not sure how the debate team is going to handle this without sounding like a bunch of homophobes. I for one am tired of hearing all the rhetoric. So let's think some more, but keep it manageable. How about you, Sebastián, any ideas?"

Sebastián places a finger to his lips. "I think I've got one that might weave together the desires of both our friends."

We all perk up to listen carefully.

"There's no need to reinvent the wheel since it's already been set in motion from the start," he says. The rest of us look confused.

Sebastián goes on: "I'm talking about the prom. There's already a prom scheduled for May, so why not insist that gay couples be allowed to attend? And better yet, we lobby to allow a couple to run for King and Queen of the prom. That would certainly challenge the heterosexist policies of this high school. It's probably a more accessible lesson for high school students than gay adoption, don't you agree, Lib?"

Lib nods his head. "Inspired." He begins to applaud.

"I have to start making my dress," Trini says.

I stare at Sebastián. I have to admit that I'm impressed. It just might work: while we inch forward toward the graduation gown, we will make an activist statement by wearing mariposa gowns, metaphorically speaking. Except for Trini—she's going to wear a dress all right.

I decide to make it official. "Sounds to me like we just resurrected the Mariposa Club," I declare. "All those in favor of pursuing this proposal?"

"Aye!" the membership cries out. It's unanimous.

"The next step is to give Boozely the heads up," I say. "But not until we figure out a plan that will make us unstoppable."

"Ab-fabby! Shall we close with our gang sign?" Trini suggests.

Sebastián follows our lead: arms crossed over the chest, thumbs locked, fingers spread open and fluttering.

Hotter

Last semester we had social studies during fifth period, which wasn't too bad because at least the material was interesting even if the teacher wasn't. I'm talking about Mr. Artnott—that's Hotnot behind his back, because he has the distinction of being the least attractive faculty member in the school—maybe in the town. He's harmless and nondescript. In fact, I always said that if he ever committed a crime, no police sketch could ever pin him down. No one likes him or dislikes him because no one really knows he exists, and that's only because he's completely upstaged by the best-looking faculty member who takes over the second semester of fifth period senior year: Mr. Trotter—that's Hotter to those of us with eyes. Unfortunately, the subject also shifts to the most boring topic known to adolescents: government.

Sebastián, Lib and I take our places near the front. Not even Sebastián is immune to the charms of the sharply-dressed man in leather suspenders and a tie that points to the lovely nub at the crotch.

"My, my, my," Sebastián says. "Things are looking better and better every day at Caliente Valley High."

"Wait until he turns around," I say. And then, as if on cue, Hotter turns around to scribble on the chalkboard. The janitor will have to haul in a trough to collect all the drooling going on in the second row.

How to describe that ass? It's not that I'm an ass guy or anything, it's just that ours has yet to inflate. We've got either skin and bone, or a tub of jelly, so when the perfect, round hard-as-a-volleyball specimen comes into view, it's tough not to appreciate it the way one appreciates Michelangelo's David, from the back, of course. So *there*, like the prized diamond in Joyería Dutton—three-dimensional but out of reach. You don't just want to touch it, you want to stick it in your mouth, show your taste buds a good time. I'd like to carry around one of those asses some day and make the boys of fifth period weak in the knees.

"I see we have a new student," Hotter says, and Sebastián wakes up from his daydream. "Mr. Sandoval, is it?"

"Yes!" Sebastián says, a little too eager.

And there's an awkward silence, an exchange of some sort between them that not everybody in the classroom notices—but I do. It's the kind of telepathy that occurs when one guy likes another and they make body contact in the realm of fantasy and imagination. It's called a virtual screw.

Okay, now I'm back to jealous. So I've been here four years and not once has Hotter even noticed that I'm alive! Make room for me on the invisible bus, Mr. Artnott! And Sebastián is in class five minutes and they're having some sort of mental love affair? Wow. This *is* something.

Hotter regains his composure and begins to lecture about the most important philosophers and thinkers who shaped the world's governments—people like Kant, Calvin and Hobbes—"Not to be confused with the comic strip!" Har har har. Sebastián actually cracks a smile at Hotter's lame attempt at a joke. The rest of us roll our eyes.

The more he talks, the less attractive Mr. Trotter becomes and suddenly he's no different that some of the jocks who throw cold water on your fiery loins as soon as they open their mouths.

The romance between Mr. Trotter and Sebastián gets a little more gross when Hotter asks the class if anyone has read any of the literature written by any of the men he just named. I wasn't really paying attention so I can't say, but Sebastián apparently wants to score all his points on his first day. He raises his hand.

"Mr. Sandoval," Mr. Trotter says, delighted.

"Machiavelli," Sebastián says. "The end justifies the means."

Mr. Trotter all but applauds when he blurts out, "Excellent!"

"I knew that," I whisper to Lib. "Lib?"

Lib simply sits there, gawking. "This is going to feed my night fantasies for at least a week," he whispers back.

No one else seems to notice or care about the love-fest going on between the teacher and the new kid, and Mr. Trotter doesn't seem to notice or care that this first day of class has turned into a dialogue while the rest of the students pass notes, text message or talk among themselves. But the real kicker comes when it's time for senior break and everyone except for Sebastián rushes out the front door.

"What's he doing in there?" I ask Lib. "Asking about extra credit already?"

"Hot," Lib says.

"Oh, please, Lib, you know there's nothing going on in there. It's like all kinds of wrong," I say, though I'm not that certain about this myself.

Lib crosses his arms and says, "How long are we going to stand here waiting for him? Break is brief and then it's time for math with Ms. Lemmons."

After a few more minutes, Sebastián comes out of the classroom, basking in an afterglow.

"It's about time," I say. "I thought I was going to need a crowbar to pry you out of Mr. Trotter's arms."

Sebastián raises his eyebrows. "Is he your boyfriend, Maui?" he asks.

I'm taken aback by the question.

He follows up with another question: "Am *I* your boyfriend?" And then goes for the kill: "So what's the problem?"

"Got you there, Maui," Lib says.

I'm suddenly suspicious of Sebastián's argumentative skills: it's like he has a degree in the Socratic method or something. And I can't help but think there's some large plot underneath it all that I have yet to uncover. It's like Machiavelli—there's a goal here, but all those steps he's taking to achieve it don't necessarily shed light on the mission to be accomplished.

"How long is the break, anyway?" Sebastián asks Lib.

"Thirty minutes," Lib says. "Trini's probably sitting at the Queer Planter, wondering where we are."

We aboutface to the Queer Planter, where, indeed, Trini awaits with her hands on her hips.

"About time," she says. "I was ready to send out a search party."

"Drama queen," Lib sing-songs.

Trini snaps back: "Oh, you hush, Limp Huarache, I'm having makeup withdrawals. Did anyone pack an extra stick of eyeliner?"

There's an ache in the back of my head, but I better get over it because right after math class I have to walk to Las Cazuelas to do a bit of homework in Papi's office and then start my shift as afternoon host. It's been a strange day, to say the least, with me ping-ponging from one emotion to the other, thanks to this new ingredient in my salsa called Sebastián. I'm quickly becoming obsessed with the guy who wants a piece of my apple pie. Geez, what's up with all the food metaphor? And then I remember: I was too embarrassed to eat my fish sandwich in front of Sebastián. I'm hungry.

We shoot the shit for the rest of the break since there isn't really time to discuss any of the important matters that were brought up that day, like crashing the prom and prying on Sebastián's "thing" for Hotter. And I kind of like it this way, tame and even-tempered.

When the bells rings, bringing an end to senior break, we separate again. Trini heads to basic math and the rest of us to college prep calculus with Ms. Lemmons—Melons to the wide-eyed straight boys. But before we walk into the room, Sebastián pulls me back.

"Hey, Maui, I was thinking maybe I could stop by at the restaurant and give you a ride home after work."

My heart skips a beat. Of course I want to say yes immediately, but there's also my father to consider. I did already spill the beans about the exchange between Sebastián and me on Three Kings Day.

"Let me just square things away with my father," I tell him. "He looks forward to our drives home together. But taking me home on a *Friday* night would work out better since I don't have school or work on Saturday. I'll let you know."

"Sure. Call me. I'll slip you my number in class. It seems appropriate to pass you a paper with digits during math, doesn't it?"

It's corny, but I like it. I smile. Mami never warned me that even making that kind of expression could freeze on my face. The parentheses around my mouth don't let up until Melons assigns homework on the first day back in school.

Mariposa Gown

Smooching Summit

Las Cazuelas is not particularly busy on a Monday evening. An occasional couple pops in here and there, but no large groups or families. In fact, there will be very little stress that week until Friday, Yolanda tells me, when all kinds of citizens of the valley get their Mexican food fix. I pretty much have the routine down after working at the restaurant only a few days and Yolanda has gotten more comfortable taking cigarette breaks about every other hour, which doesn't bother me since I have no reason to take a cigarette break myself: I don't have a cell phone or a boyfriend to fight with.

The dust settles at school as well, where Sebastián awes the girls at lunchtime with his homemade gourmet meals stuffed into the little tin canisters, and where he seduces every faculty member on his course schedule, including What's-his-name, the new chemistry teacher. Other students don't show much resentment toward him since it's clear that when he takes all the attention there's less pressure to hide from the teachers when they ask a question or invite volunteers to the chalkboard. Sometimes Lib, our homegrown genius, beats him to the punch, but when that happens, Sebastián graciously concedes, which endears him to the teachers even more.

It becomes a private joke between us when he asks me every day at the end of math class if he can carry my books home for me, which is code for *Can I drive you home tonight?* and each time I say, “Not until Friday.”

When Friday actually arrives, I feel a tingling sensation in my stomach all day. I’m so lovesick that I even ignore the moment when Mr. Trotter and Sebastián get into some disagreement about imperialism. I can’t even say who’s on what side or what the whole beef is about, but Mr. Trotter does manage to get so flushed and excited that if I didn’t know any better, I’d say this is how a government teacher gets his rocks off.

When I arrive at Las Cazuelas that afternoon, I’m delighted to see all the new shelving that has gone up in what will become the Mexican curio market, where Lib’s going to work. In about a week or so he starts his training and the grand opening is on February second. *Fabulous!*

“Hello, handsome,” Yolanda croons from the hostess station.

“Hello, beautiful,” I croon back. “Why are we in such a good mood?”

“Because Mr. Sandoval’s coming in tonight,” she says.

I grin. “Whoa.”

“What whoa?”

I shake my head. “Nothing. Just wondering if this means Mr. Gutiérrez and Mr. Benson will be expected to stay late tonight.”

“Well, I’m sure they won’t mind. They sure had a blast last week.”

Yolanda’s right. I suppose I shouldn’t worry. Still, I decide to pay Papi a visit at his office on my way to the locker room to change into my guayabera. I need to tell him about Sebastián anyway.

"Knock, knock," I say.

My father looks up from behind a stack of paperwork. "Maui, come in, come in."

"Don't mean to bother you," I say. "I just wanted to let you know I'm getting a ride home tonight, but I can change that if you need me to drive again."

My father waves his hand across his face. "No," he says. "That was a one-time thing. You know, spur of the moment. I don't think it's going to become a habit, although I do enjoy Mr. Sandoval's company. He's a very intelligent and sophisticated man."

"I'm sure he is," I say. "He's certainly scoring high marks with the locals, isn't he? I mean, bringing jobs to the valley and all."

"He's like a rainy day after a drought, that's for sure," he says.

"Papi," I stammer. "I'll be spending some time with Sebastián Sandoval tonight."

My father freezes. He looks up at me. "Okay," he says finally.

"You hesitated," I say.

"No," he says. "I didn't hesitate, I just had to let it sink in. You're a big boy, I trust you and I believe you know how to take care of yourself."

I'm feeling a little nervous all of a sudden. What neither of us wants to admit is that there's a possibility that this time I might give in to Sebastián's advances. And I want to reassure my father that nothing of the sort will happen, but I'm not too sure about it either.

"I can take care of myself," I say. "And he's a nice guy, underneath that—" I stop myself. I was about to say "costume," what I told Sebastián about Trini and Lib. I guess that takes me one step closer to the real guy.

"Underneath that what?" Papi asks.

"Nothing," I say. "Just thinking aloud, that's all."

My father takes a deep breath and I know it's going to get nice and awkward. "You know, son. I'm new to this gay thing myself," he says. "If you were straight I might be able to give you better dating advice because I went through it once. But letting you go out with another young man confuses me a little about what I can say to let you know that I love you and care about you and hope that you will have a safe and wonderful time. Emphasis on the safe."

Oh, my God. He's putting condoms in my purse. I let him off gently.

"I understand, Papi. And thank you."

Without even blinking, I hustle over to the locker room, change and then take my place next to Yolanda.

"What's the matter with you?" she asks.

"My father started talking to me about protection," I say.

Yolanda sighs. "Poor thing. A decade into the twenty-first century and there's still no easy way to broach the subject. I hope you were kind."

"Exceedingly," I say.

Yolanda bends down to plant a kiss on my forehead. "Good boy."

The evening passes without anything particularly interesting transpiring, except when the shipment of merchandise from Mexico gets rolled into the market. Mr. Benson and my father open up a few of the boxes to admire the colorful contents: papier-mâché dolls, little wooden animals with toothpick horns and tails, and an array of Mexican toys like tops painted forest green and tin cars that make men like Papi nostalgic for the homeland. They approve of the merchandise and then decide this is yet another occasion to celebrate, so Mr. Benson orders two shots of tequila, and that's when Mr. Sandoval arrives, which is Mr. Benson's cue to invite him to partake. Yolanda and I don't even bother to step in and escort Mr. Sandoval to his table since Mr. Benson and Mr. Gutiérrez have already taken over.

"Three, apparently, is not a crowd," says Yolanda, and then she's off to take a cigarette break.

At about ten, my shift is over. Yolanda leaves before me, however, since I have to wait for Sebastián. He's not late, just not early, so I sit in the waiting area and pull out the heavy weight around my neck, *East of Eden*.

"How far along are you?" a voice asks. I smile.

Sebastián looks great. He smells great. He has slicked the sides of his black hair back, which allows his pale ears to step forward. Easier access for nibbling.

"Let me just see how my father's doing," I say. "Your father's here too, you know."

"I know," he says. "I think he's enjoying his Friday night outings to Las Cazuelas, though he's not allowed to get drunk tonight. He drove his own car."

We walk to the back table, where the three drinking buddies are playing dominoes. Mr. Benson is particularly tickled to see that Sebastián and I have forged our own friendship.

"You boys enjoy yourselves," he says. "I've got about five nieces and two daughters out and about, so behave! I say we toast to that: to youth and the adventures that only come once in a lifetime!"

My father and Mr. Sandoval raise their glasses, though they don't seem to share in Mr. Benson's reverie. In fact, they look at each other, as if for a moment each can read the same concerns in the other man's eyes.

"Be home at a decent hour," Mr. Sandoval tells Sebastián.

"Stay out of trouble," Papi says to me.

"Yes, sir," Sebastián and I say in unison. We say our goodbyes and before we know it, we're in his car, kissing.

"Wait," I say, pushing Sebastián back. "Not here."

"You're right. Too tacky to make out in a parking lot. Where to? Palm Springs again?"

"Please, no," I say. "There's actually another option, not far from here, but it's a spot reserved for more special occasions."

"Point the way," Sebastián says. We rush up to the Chiriaco Summit, a.k.a. Smooching Summit.

Isaac and I never came up to the summit. It was one of our many unspoken agreements about keeping the friendship platonic. But no such deal has been struck between Sebastián and me, though I'm proceeding with caution. I'm not worried about what the straight kids in school will say, or even about my father or my teachers, but Trini and Lib—that's another matter.

There are already a few cars parked at the summit, each a polite distance from any other and all of them facing the breathtaking view of the valley. I can see why this height would inspire smooching. Floating over the desert as it shimmers with lights and stretches out like the glamorous train on the gown of an empress makes a person want to mark the occasion somehow, punctuate it with a kiss. I reach for Sebastián's hand in the dark and he intertwines my fingers into his.

After a few seconds of simply sitting there, staring out, he leans over and pecks my cheek. It feels a little more restrained this time, not the aggressive tongue-wrestle we had last week, but I figure he's taking it slow tonight, which I can appreciate. Another minute passes, but nothing else. Is this it? Or maybe he wants me to make the move this time. I hate the mind-reading game. Well, I take a chance and launch my face into his. He stops me.

"Can we just sit here a little longer," he says.

"What?" I'm confused.

"Sorry. It's not that I don't want to make out with you or anything, but I'm a bit distracted."

"I see," I say. "You're seeing someone else?"

"Someone else?" Sebastián says, scoffing. "Like who? Mr. Trotter?"

"Out of your lips, not mine," I say.

"Give me a break, Maui, how can I be seeing our high school teacher? He's like twenty years older than we are. I know he's getting off on it, so I let him. We too will be queens pushing forty one of these days and we'll be begging to get some attention from boys half our age. It's how it goes."

I furrow my forehead. "So you're flirting with him as a favor to his ego?"

"Yeah," he says. "What's wrong with that?"

I don't want to bring up the whole Isaac-Armando thing, though that seems to make a bit more sense now. I think.

"You know, insecurity is an ugly trait," Sebastián says.

"And so is not being yourself." Sebastián is taken aback, but I go on. "I think it's sad the lengths you go to so that people will like you. You try to impress everyone by reading big books and bringing fancy food to lunch and parading your wheels around the entire school. Why can't you just be who you really are, without the smoke and mirrors?"

"This *is* who I am," Sebastián says.

I shake my head. "No it's not. Those are the things you collect around you—material things and props. And you didn't even buy them yourself, your father did, so it's not even anything you achieved on your own."

"Okay, now you're being mean."

"You're the mean one," I say, holding my stance. "Playing with people's emotions like that."

"Whose? Trotter's?"

"And anyone else you come across. Including me," I say.

Suddenly I want to change the name of this place to Smearing Summit, because that's what I'm doing to him and I can't stop myself.

Mariposa Gown

"Maybe I should drive you home," Sebastián says.

"Maybe you should," I say.

And just as quickly as we ascended to the summit, we descend, though I could have kicked myself in the ass and dropped down much quicker. When we reach the bottom, I run my hands over my head.

"Wait," I say. "This is all wrong. Pull over."

"That's all right, pal," Sebastián says. "I want to spare you any more grief."

"Please, Sebastián." The timbre in my voice convinces him to slow down and come to a stop at the side of the road.

I let a few minutes pass, enough for both of us to cool off, before I speak. "I'm sorry. I realize that you asked me to listen to you and then I derailed the whole conversation into something else. Something about me and not about you."

Sebastián takes a deep breath. When he exhales the scent of mint reaches my nose and I resist the urge to lunge at him. Not now, not yet. We're making up first, and then we get to make out.

"I'm sorry I'm touchy tonight," he says. "I'm feeling out of my element. You and Trini and Lib have been great to me all week, but I'm still feeling disoriented, leaving the old high school behind. And then there's the whole issue between my parents."

"They're divorced, right?"

Sebastián shakes his head. "Officially, as of today. That's why my father went to Las Cazuelas—to celebrate. But now my mother wants to take me with her. She's upset that my father made me move down here with him. And since the house in Orange County has been sold she's moving to New York City."

I panic. "You're not leaving, are you? You just got here."

"She really wants me to go, and she says she can force my father to let me go, but I don't want to aggravate the hostility, it's been so painful already," he says. "Whatever I decide I'll end up hurting someone's feelings. It's not fair."

When a tear runs down Sebastián's cheek, I think it's the most beautiful light I've seen tonight. This is the real Sebastián, just as scared and vulnerable as the rest of us. I reach over and pull him towards me. I don't want to make out with him, I want to comfort him. And it could have been a wonderful extended moment of affection if the town sheriff hadn't come along to blast his killjoy lights at us.

"What now?" I say, separating from Sebastián.

The sheriff gets out of his squad car and walks over cautiously. "Good evening," Sheriff Johnson calls out. He shines the light on my face and recognizes me. "Maui," he says. "Car trouble?"

"No, sir. My friend and I were just taking in the night. We came down from the summit and thought we'd take in the view from down here."

"The summit, huh?" he says, which means that he knows we were being naughty. He turns to Sebastián. "License and registration, please."

"Sheriff Johnson," I protest.

Sebastián waves his hand at me. "He's just doing his job, Maui." He shows the sheriff his paperwork.

"Mr. Sandoval from the good old O.C." the sheriff comments. "A ways from home, are we?"

I'm mortified. Here I am trying to prove to Sebastián that we're an honest, hard-working town and here's the sheriff, talking like a hick. What's he going to do next, search the car?

"Do you mind if I take a look around in there?" he asks.

My jaw drops open. "Sheriff Johnson," I say. "You know who I am, you know my father. What's this all about? This is Sebastián Sandoval, the son of the big boss over at Sandoval Construction."

"Thank you, Maui," the sheriff says. "I'd appreciate your cooperation just about now. Young man, do you mind if I take a look around?"

"I do mind, sir," Sebastián says.

"Sebastián," I say, shocked at how quickly the tide can turn. "That's wrong. You have to give him permission to search, there's nothing to find in here, right?"

"It doesn't matter," Sebastián says. "It's the principle of the thing. There's no reason for the sheriff to search my car without a warrant. If he's got a reason to suspect anything, then perhaps he should arrest me."

My mouth goes dry. "Are you kidding me? This is the town sheriff. This is my friend Maddy's father!"

"Actually, he's right, Maui," Sheriff Johnson says. "I have no reason to search this car. Though it sounds to me like I'll have to keep an eye out for this young man in the future. I could cite him for illegal parking, but I won't. I'll show him a little Caliente Valley hospitality. As for you, Maui, I'm disappointed you're keeping this kind of company. As a father, I'm not sure I won't speak to your father about this. For your own good, of course."

Sebastián, welcome to small town justice.

"You two can go now," the sheriff says. "But drive carefully."

When Sebastián turns the ignition on and shifts to drive, he's about to say something but I stop him.

"Just shut up and take me home," I say.

Bad Boys and Mean Men

Before my father leaves for work Saturday morning, he calls me into the living room for a chat. He just got off the phone with Sheriff Johnson. I take a seat on the living room couch. I know what's coming.

"This puts us all in a compromising situation," Papi says.

Ooh, when he gets all formal like that I know it's bad. He paces about a few times with his left hand on his hip. Mickey watches from the kitchen with a half-eaten bagel in her hand. I haven't even brushed my teeth, so I feel as if I've got last night's bitterness still lingering in my mouth.

"I don't have time right now to wrap my brain around this," he says. "But for now, you're grounded."

"Grounded!" I blurt out. "Why am I grounded? I didn't do anything. Didn't Sheriff Johnson tell you that I was the one pleading with Sebastián to cooperate?"

"Yes, he did. Okay, you're not grounded. I don't know! I think I'm going to have to speak with Mr. Sandoval, though. He should know his son's going to get himself into a heap of trouble slinging around that little rich boy attitude around here. Until then, stay away from the kid. No calls, no visits, no anything. Understood?" My father does that parental pointing gesture to punctuate each word at the end of his list of no's.

"What about in school?" I ask. "We've got like identical schedules."

"That's different," he says. "But no more riding in the car with him. Who knows what he's hiding. You know, Maui, you don't want to have a criminal record before you graduate from high school. This could ruin your life!"

He grabs his car keys and slams the door shut behind him when he's out of the house. I know he's not really angry at me, he's angry at the situation, how he allowed all of this to happen. I mean, I didn't invite Mr. Sandoval and his son to come have dinner at Las Cazuelas—Mr. Benson and Mr. Gutiérrez did.

"Tsk, tsk, tsk," Mickey chimes in behind me. I roll my eyes. "Maui's got a thing for the bad boy."

"He's not a bad boy." I say. "He's having a hard time adjusting, that's all."

"That's a bad boy, all right: a hard time adjusting, probably comes from a broken home. Am I right? Thought so."

I turn to face Mickey. "Okay, Dr. Phil, and how do you propose I help?"

Mickey's face changes. "Help? Maui, you stay away from him, just like Papi said." She walks over and sits beside me on the couch. She puts her arm around me. "Look, I know you like him, and deep down inside I'm sure he's a good person. But you have to think about *your* well-being too. Whatever problems he has are bigger than both of you. If he's going to get help it's going to come from a professional, not from his seventeen-year-old boyfriend."

"I'm not his boyfriend," I say.

"You know what I mean," Mickey says.

I could protest more strongly, but last night's incident has given me doubts. Sebastián doesn't challenge authority, he craves its graces. Why else has he been sucking up to every teacher at the school? Maybe there was a reason he didn't want Sheriff Johnson to search his car? Principles, my faggotty brown ass! I guess the only way to find out is to ask him for the truth.

"Hey, Mickey, can I get a ride to Trini's?" I ask.

"Sure, squirt," she says. "Just be ready in an hour. I've got to meet Sandra and Janet at whatever's left of the mall by the time we get there. We're planning a baby shower for Maddy. Which, by the way, you have to help out with, since we'll be holding it at Las Cazuelas."

"No problem," I say. Baby showers. Go figure.

When I get to Trini's, the Glamorous Grotto looks like it's been struck by a hurricane—hurricane Ramos, that is. The furniture's intact, but the frilly curtains over the only window in the shed have been yanked down and articles of clothing lie scattered about, the most delicate items torn to shreds. Trini sits on the floor with makeup smeared on her face, her arms wrapped around her knees.

I approach slowly. "Hey, are you okay?"

She sniffles. I look around for a rag. There are too many rags around but none that are useful. So I reach into my pocket for a tissue. I hand it to her.

"Thanks." She uses it to wipe the streaks of lipstick across her cheeks and forehead.

"Maybe you should come back to live with us," I say.

Trini holds out her arms and I help her off the floor. "It's not as bad as it looks," she says.

My eyes widen as I take in the room once more. "It's not? It looks kind of bleak to me."

Trini comes up to me and gives me a tight hug. My eyes begin to tear.

"You're always so good to me, Passion Flower," she says. "That's why you'll always be my favorite."

"Do you want to tell me what happened?" I say. We clear out the divan and sit.

Trini takes a deep breath. "He's really becoming unpredictable. It used to be that what I wore or how I walked or even how I talked would bother him, but now I don't know what will set him off. I guess he was looking over the grocery bill and he noticed I sneaked in a magazine. I mean, can you blame me? Ricky Martin on the cover! I thought it would make a nice addition to the Glamorous Grotto gallery. It used to be over there, remember?"

She points to a wall that now stands bare. But the sheets of crumpled paper with the crushed faces of our favorite hunks are strewn all over the floor. "And then he came at me with the lipstick. It's my fault for leaving it lying around."

"No, Trini. It's not your fault he attacked you, that's ridiculous."

"Well, I shouldn't have put that magazine in the shopping cart. It cost almost five dollars. We don't have that kind of money to spend on garbage."

"Is that your father talking or you?" I ask.

Trini lowers her head and starts to cry again.

Once the tears dry, the clean-up begins. There's very little we can salvage in terms of the clothing that's been torn up, even if we were expert seamstresses, so all of those items go into the trash. The posters and the sheets out of the glossy gossip magazines are useless now, but these I pick up myself since it's too painful for Trini to throw away her collection. By the end, the Glamorous Grotto only looks a little less cluttered—a clean slate for Trini to start decorating from scratch.

"Are you thirsty? I've got some apple juice that we can drink," Trini says. "But let me change into something a little more fabulous first."

I smile, knowing that she's back to her old self as she wraps a shawl and dons a large black hat with a red ribbon. She pours the apple juice into the china teacups and arranges them delicately on a serving tray. It's tea time, apparently.

"You know, I've been thinking more and more about Sebastián's idea to hijack the straight prom," Trini says. "I think it's the only thing that will get me through these final months at home."

Sebastián. I want to let Trini in on what happened, but I want this day to be about her. Besides, Papi said it was okay if Sebastián and I crossed paths in school, and technically, the Mariposa Club's prom plot is school-related.

"Yes, we should definitely pursue it, though we have to give Boozely fair warning," I say. "He's not going to like it but I don't think he has a choice. We'll let Lib deal with the legal aspect of it, since he's more informed about that than anyone of us."

"I think it'll be a fantastic way to end our four years of high school hell," Trini says.

"It wasn't that bad. Besides, it's also four years of high school friendship."

Trini smiles at me. "Oh, my Passion Flower," she says, stroking my cheek. "I'm glad one of us can see a tinsel lining on this dark cloud."

"And what do you intend to do after graduation?" I ask, finally. She's been hinting at this for days.

"What I've been wanted to do all along: get my cosmetology certificate, move to Palm Springs and do hair and nails," she says. "Anything's better than sticking around here. I've already done some research. I can start as early as June and be ready to file and highlight by Christmas. *Financial aid available for those who qualify!*"

Mariposa Gown

I take her hands to offer some encouragement. "That's a wonderful start," I say. "Though you might think about college later."

Trini shakes her head. "Oh, Maui," she says. "School is for nerds like you and Lib. No offense. But I don't have the grades or the desire to pursue college. It's not for everybody, you know that."

"I know," I say. "But don't just assume you're never going to go."

"I won't," she says, but I don't believe her. Still, I need to support my friend, so I give her another hug.

It's in this pose that Mr. Ramos finds us when he charges in.

"What's going on here?" he asks. "Trinidad, take off that ridiculous get-up."

"Mr. Ramos," I say. "There's nothing going on here, sir. There's no reason for you to get angry."

Mr. Ramos doesn't look at me. Instead he drills holes into Trini. "Trinidad, your friend needs to go home. You have to go with your mother to Aunt Carmen's doctor's appointment. Did you hear me?!"

When Mr. Ramos barks this last sentence, Trini and I both jump, and that's when I lose it.

"Stop yelling at her!" I say, not believing I'm acting so disrespectfully toward an adult. An echo of Sebastián's confrontation with Sheriff Johnson comes to mind.

"Maui," Trini says. "That's my father."

"And *he* is not a *she*, young man," Mr. Ramos says. "You and the fat kid have been cheerleading this act from the beginning. Do you understand that you're just making my son susceptible to hatred?"

"And the only person I see exercising that hatred is you, Mr. Ramos," I say.

This flusters Trini's father. He gets all red-faced and then stops himself from saying anything else, so he turns around and stomps out of the Glamorous Grotto.

"Well, that showed him," I say to Trini.

Trini looks at me with disbelief. "I can't frickin' believe you just did that."

"No need to thank me. He had it coming."

"Thank you?" Trini says. "I should slap you!"

Now it's my turn to express disbelief. I stand up for her and now she's mad at me?

"I just told you we're going through some difficult times, Maui," Trini says. "He doesn't mean to hurt me. Not really."

I want to stop now, but I can't, so I keep at it: "He's been hurting you for years. What was his excuse before your mother lost her job and they went broke? He's abusing you, can't you see that?"

"I love him, Maui. As imperfect as he is he's still my father," Trini says. "You have no right to insult him like that!"

"I'm sorry," I say.

"Too late, jerk-off!" She points at the door. "Now leave before I really say something I'll regret."

Dazed, I walk out of the Glamorous Grotto, past Aunt Carmen's, and head to the Lame View Mall, where I hope to locate my sister. But I don't, so after about half an hour of walking around aimlessly, I sit down beneath the glass shelter of the bus stop, where the ghost of Tony Sánchez still lingers. When the tears begin to pour, I'm confused about what I'm crying about because there's so much pain in me right now, from Sebastián's betrayal, to Trini's anger and abusive relationship with Mr. Ramos, to the memory of Tony. When the bus arrives and takes me away, I turn around the way I did that time when I left Tony sitting there, looking at his girlfriend's picture. I see him on the bench again, in peace now, maybe even happy, because his troubles are over. It's the rest of us, those he left behind, who still have to battle the hard times.

Mariposa Gown

Incomplete Portraits

On Monday, neither Sebastián nor Trini show up to school, which wouldn't be a big deal on any other day except that today is when the clubs gather for the yearbook photos. The Mariposa Club will be weakly represented by only two of its members. I don't wear anything special, but Lib must have plundered Celie's closet over the weekend because he shows up in full Goth regalia: a black frock with a leather coat and a belt with large skulls around it, boots with elevated heels and a cluster of spikes jutting out from the ankles, and a top hat with a red piece of veil wrapped around it. And to complete the look, he brings another one of his homemade Gothic skeleton ballerinas that he lets hang from his wrist. He even switched his lip ring from black to something a little more noticeable in blood red. In those boots, he's taller than me for once.

"You know," I say as we sit across from each other in the library during study hour. "We're not getting our picture taken until senior break. You're going to drag all that gear around the entire day?"

Lib shrugs his shoulders. "I have to. You think I can just take this off and put it back on at the drop of a ghoulish hat? It takes time to pull my Goth self together."

Mr. Gump stares in awe from a distance. *Now* he's seen everything.

For the most part, the kids and teachers at school are used to seeing Lib's Goth wear, but even this is overdoing it, which provokes more than a few snide remarks. Lib takes it in stride.

"Halloween already?" one of the tough guys says as he walks past our table.

Lib doesn't hold his tongue: "Parole already?"

But even without Sebastián and Trini, we have to move forward on our prom plot.

"I have an appointment to see Mr. Beasley after we take our club photo," I say. I hesitate to ask Lib to join me, but decide right away that we have nothing to lose. "You're coming, right?"

"Right," Lib says. "I want to come say hello to the administration secretaries anyway. I can't wait for them to see me!"

I grin. For the rest of study hour I tell Lib about the incident with Sebastián and Sheriff Johnson, and then about Mr. Ramos and me, and though it doesn't surprise me it doesn't cease to disappoint me what a great distance exists between grown-ups and teenagers. The grown-ups really have no excuse—they were teenagers once. They should know about rebellion. We teenagers don't rebel because we want to, but because we have to.

"What do you think Sebastián was hiding? Drugs?" Lib whispers.

I shrug. "I don't know. I'm not allowed to speak with him over the phone so I haven't had time to ask him directly. I was hoping he'd tell me today."

"He called you over the weekend at least?"

I nod. “He left two messages. I was half expecting him to show up at brunch yesterday but he didn’t.”

“When you do find out, Maui, I hope you’ll make the right decision,” Lib says. “We can’t have junkies in the Mariposa Club.”

“I would hardly refer to Sebastián as a junkie,” I say.

“I’m just saying. And what are we going to do about Trini? We can’t just sit back and let her father beat the crap out of her whenever he wants.”

I sigh. “I don’t know,” I say, my voice trembling a bit. “It’s complicated. She wants us to stay out of it, but it doesn’t look like she’s doing anything to stop him.”

Lib leans in closer and says, “I’ve read about these things *online*. Many gay men become trapped in abusive relationships because they love their abusers—they confuse violence for affection.”

“This is a father/daughter relationship,” I tell Lib.

“Doesn’t matter. Spouses, lovers, fathers/daughters: the dynamics are similar.”

“Regardless,” I say. “Until Trini’s ready to get help I’m not sure what kind of intervention we can provide without getting Mr. Ramos into trouble and getting Trini mad at us.”

“Maybe that’s what needs to happen. She may hate us for it, but in the long run she’ll be glad we had the courage to do what we did.”

“I don’t know, Lib.” I say. And I really don’t know. Things like these aren’t in the gay kid handbook. I want to do the right thing, but the right thing is called the wrong thing by the parties directly affected. Well, yet another piece of evidence that there’s no black or white, just another blurry shade of hurt.

When we get to the gym during senior break, the one kid who hasn’t seen Lib has his chance to take a swipe: “Which club is this? The Rocky Horror Picture Club?”

Mariposa Gown

Lib lets him have it as we take our turn in front of the camera. "It's the Taxidermy Club," he says. "Through which end do *you* want to get stuffed?"

Because Lib is larger than life in his extravagant outfit, I disappear standing next to him. I can't even compete with the Gothic skeleton ballerina. If anything, I'll look like the photographer's assistant who just happened to get caught in the shot since Lib is all front and center.

"Say cheese," the photographer says.

"Black lipstick," Lib says. The word *cheese* gets caught in my teeth, so I swallow it back. It's all Lib all up in here today!

I'm saddened by the fact that this is not going to reflect the true image and history of the Mariposa Club. Without Maddy, who named us, without Isaac or Trini, our other founding members, and without Sebastián, our newest member, this photograph is going to look more like the Goth Club and its one admirer. And that's exactly how we arrive at the administration office, where Lib causes a stir of admiration as we wait our turn to see Boozely.

"Boys," he says when he finally sticks his head out of his office. Even his comb-over looks shocked when he takes in Lib. "Come in."

"Thank you, Mr. Beasley," I say. "We won't take up more of your time since we have math class. In fact, it already started."

"Sorry," he says. "That's my fault. I'll make sure and hand you tardy slips before you leave. Well, what can I do for you, boys? We're throwing a parade of some kind?"

Lib winces. "Actually, sir," he says. "Today's club portrait day for the yearbook. Hence the fierce outfit. What we came to talk about is a whole other matter."

"Go on," he says.

"Well," I say. "We understand that as graduating seniors we have every right to attend the senior prom, and we intend to. Except that we believe it is also within our rights as students at Caliente Valley High School to submit our nominations for Prom King and Queen at the dance."

Mr. Beasley looks like he's losing his patience. "Okay," he says. "I don't see what's wrong with any of this. Has someone from the prom committee denied your nomination?"

"We're getting there, sir," I say. "You see..." I want to find the right words, but Lib seems to misinterpret my pause as hesitation, so he blurts it out.

"We're nominating two queens," Lib says.

"You mean two young women?" Mr. Beasley asks.

Lib chuckles. "No, not two lesbians. Two young men—gay boys."

It suddenly dawns on Mr. Beasley what the complication's going to be. "Ah, I see," he says, suddenly out of breath.

I can tell he wants to reach down to one of the drawers and take a swig of his whiskey bottle, or whatever it is he's rumored to keep hidden in there.

After a brief silence, the principal speaks out: "I suppose I won't be able to stop this, just like I couldn't stop you from establishing that Mariposa Club of yours, or setting up that table on campus, where you passed out literature and got yourself into a bit of trouble. All of our students are entitled to exercise the few freedoms we sanction here. But I warn you, Mr. Gutiérrez and Mr. García: I don't want this to distract the other students from having a problem-free prom. *They* have a right to that as well."

"With all due respect, Mr. Beasley," Lib says. "If you or any of the students have a problem with gay students attending the prom, then that's something you and the other students have to work out."

"I'm not saying I have a problem with you, Mr. García, don't you *dare* put words in my mouth," Mr. Beasley says. I have a feeling in my gut this isn't going to end well. "I'm just saying I would appreciate if you participated without causing distractions or deliberately sabotaging anybody else's fun for the sake of making some political statement. Proms are for fun, for punctuating the end of four years with a little music and dancing. It's not the place for speeches or protests."

"I beg to differ, sir," Lib says. Now I'm squirming in my seat. "And you know that I have the support of the gay and lesbian associations of southern California—most of them know me. Not to mention my parents. The last thing you want is for Mr. and Mrs. García to come around here again."

"I think it's time for you two to get to math class," Mr. Beasley says.

"I think so too, sir," I say. "Thank you for your time."

We pick up our tardy slips and make our way to the final class of the day.

"You're not mad at me, are you, Maui?" Lib asks.

"No," I say, remembering the time when it was Trini and me at the principal's office—a meeting that didn't go so well either. But this is different. Lib is right.

"I'm actually sad, not angry," I say.

Lib pats me on the shoulder and says, "Well, don't you worry, Maui. We may not be able to change Boozely, but who knows? We might be able to teach a few of the kids around here some tolerance."

I stop. "Is that what we're here for, Lib? To teach lessons? I thought we were here to learn."

"Hmm," Lib says. "You're getting cold feet about the whole thing? No reason to be scared, Maui. In a few days Trini and Sebastián will get their acts together and rejoin the club. And then it'll really feel like a group effort."

Lib doesn't understand me this time, but I let it go. We've got math class to attend. We've got to shove Lib's overdone outerwear into one of those desks. Even though most of the students have already seen him, Lib's entrance still causes a distraction, which displeases Mrs. Lemmons. She waits for us to get settled, which takes longer than expected, before she continues her lessons on algorithms.

What I really want to tell Lib is that maybe all this effort isn't really worth it. So we'll amuse and maybe shock a few faces in the crowd, but then what? Is this really something that's going to resonate for many proms after? The fact that Lib can walk around looking the way he does only shows that we're not that interesting anymore. Maybe we should be focusing on making ourselves better people instead on imposing that expectation on others.

"Psst! Goth kid," a kid whispers from the back row. "Whose skeleton is that? Your pet hamster's?"

I can't resist. I turn around and say, "A gerbil's. That's how we pulled it out of your ass!"

Mariposa Gown

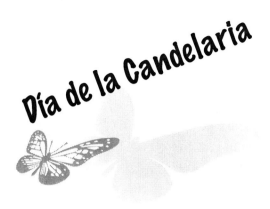

Día de la Candelaria

Trini just doesn't bother showing up at school. She doesn't return my phone calls and she doesn't answer when I knock on the door to the Glamorous Grotto. Each time I show up, I sense Mr. Ramos peeping through the window from Aunt Carmen's, and a few times I have the urge to moon him, but that would be beyond disrespectful and immature. I know Trini's in there: I can hear her boom box playing Lila Downs, which means she's melancholy. She's probably dressed up as Frida Kahlo, waving the bottle of apple juice as if it were tequila. After a couple of minutes of waiting and confirming that she's alive, I leave without saying anything to Trini's parents. They know what's up.

Sebastián on the other hand, does show up to classes after a two-day absence and doesn't say anything about the exchange with the sheriff, or my long silence over the weekend, or even about what he has doing for the past few days. For him it's just business as usual, charming the pants off of everyone. Sometimes he'll join Lib and me for lunch, but even those moments have turned into small talk about class or homework, nothing emotionally charged or relevant to the Mariposa Club. We decide it's better to wait until Trini comes back since she's an integral part of the plan.

At Las Cazuelas, we're getting the Mexican curio market ready for the grand opening on Groundhog Day—I mean—*Día de la Candelaria*. There won't be any actual liquor for sale, but there are plenty of tequila-flavored lollipops, and a few miniature bottles as part of curio gift buckets. Frida is overly represented, but she's all the rage nowadays. Lib sets up everything from Frida t-shirts to Frida mouse pads and earrings. He even made a place for his Gothic skeleton ballerina, whom he named Frida, on the counter. Frida hangs with her legs crossed from the counter lamp.

Lib gets particular pleasure in setting up the Day of the Dead figurines, from the wooden caskets to the skeleton dioramas. "They're, like, folk Gothic," he says.

One of the cashiers at Las Cazuelas comes in to give Lib some quick lessons on operating the credit card machine, though he suspects that this will mostly be a nickel and dime operation, what with Mexican candies that go for a quarter and magnets that don't run over a buck fifty. No one says anything to Lib about his wardrobe. Characteristically, he has chosen to sport a black guayabera and a hat with a skull patch on the front, which makes him fit right in with the assortment of Day of the Dead products. As I suspected, this is a perfect job for Lib.

Two days later: the grand opening. Since nothing much goes on, culturally speaking, in our town besides the high school theater productions and football, there's an immediate buzz on our *Día de la Candelaria* celebration.

Lib is in his element, ringing up the merchandise that seems to tap into every Mexican's sense of nostalgia. The wooden yo-yos and *lotería* games quickly fly off the shelves, and every woman wants her Frida Kahlo charm bracelet. Mr. Benson stands at the entrance welcoming everyone into the shop and a ballet folklórico from the local elementary school gets the festivities going with a folk dance from Veracruz. The mariachi is set to arrive later in the evening, and Mr. Gutiérrez is giddy with delight that this celebration has packed the house. Yolanda and I, though happy for our bosses, work double-time ushering parties of customers through the crowded restaurant. The only time I see a genuine smile on her face is when Mr. Sandoval shows up with his crew of secretaries, including Maddy, to a special Friday night dinner. The complimentary dessert is *rosca*, a large donut-looking thing that, technically, should have been offered on Three Kings Day, but no one seems to mind. It's free and sugary and tastes to die for with a cup of hot chocolate. Tonight is just another excuse to party. Meanwhile, for the rest of the country, the little rodent saw its shadow, so it's six more weeks of winter.

Since the restaurant is one confusion of bodies, I'm unaware of when exactly Sebastián makes his entrance, but he's standing inside the curio market, absently admiring a pair of clay salt-and-pepper shakers in the shapes of a devil and an angel.

When we eventually make eye contact he blows me a kiss, which makes me blush.

"He's certainly too young for me," Yolanda says. "So I take it that was meant for you?"

"It's complicated," I say.

"It always is, Maui," she says, and she's off to guide a family of five to a table.

When Yolanda returns, she suggests that I take my cigarette break. For once I agree to it. I make my way out the front door and I don't need to look back to know that Sebastián is following me. I walk to the side of restaurant, where Yolanda hides from the customers during her breaks.

"Hey," Sebastián says.

"Hey," I answer back. "My father better not see us talking. I could get into trouble."

"You talk to me at school," he says.

"I know," I say. I keep my hands in my pocket. "But that's different."

"Your father called my father about the incident with the sheriff," Sebastián says.

I shake my head. "I was wondering about that. Sorry."

"Not your fault. He's just being a good parent, that's all. So was my father when he took my car privileges away. And since I refused to take the bus I missed class for two days before he agreed to let me have the car to ride to school at least. Childish, huh?"

"You said it." I have the urge to roll my eyes. How offensive for him to have to stoop to taking the bus to school. Geez, some of us don't even have cars. Then I ask: "So how did you get here tonight? You had a hunger strike until your father let you have your Friday nights back?"

"*Touché,*" he says. "I deserved that. But not really. I don't have my Friday nights back. I told him I owed some people an apology. I drove to the sheriff's office to grovel, and now I'm here to apologize to you."

I have nothing else to entertain myself with so I start chewing on my fingernail, which I pull out of my mouth each time I want to say something. "I accept your apology." I say. "Though I do need to know something. And I want you to tell me the truth."

"Did I have any drugs in the car?" he says.

I nod. "Well, did you?"

"Not really. I had a whiskey flask I took from my father's liquor cabinet. It was stuffed in the glove compartment."

Underage drinking. Certainly nothing new to Sheriff Johnson, but not something I want to get busted for.

"Were you expecting me to drink with you or something? Were you drinking before you picked me up?"

Sebastián laughs nervously. "Wow," he says. "You're prying more than Sheriff Johnson did. No and no. I usually sip from it in the driveway before I walk in the door. It's tough to face my father, you know. He's been hitting the bottle a lot more since the divorce. And even though he probably wishes I were a straight boy, he's also afraid to lose me to my mother."

I turn toward the restaurant as if I have X-ray vision and can see Mr. Sandoval waving the server over for margarita pitcher refills at his table. It's kind of ironic that Sebastián uses alcohol to avoid thinking about his father's alcoholism.

"Have you decided if that's what you're going to do? Join your mother in New York City?" I ask, hoping that he'll give me the right answer. Despite everything I want him around.

"I don't think so," he says. I let out a discreet sigh of relief. "Besides," he continues. "I'm warming up to this place, and to the Mariposa Club. It's already February. Before we know it it's March, then April, then May, and then we graduate and take off to our respective destinations. I have a feeling that by then my father will be ready to let me go, but not now. He's lonely."

"The most powerful man in the Caliente Valley feels lonely?" I say, incredulously.

"Believe it," Sebastián says. "Why else do you think he comes here every Friday night to party. He wants to be among friends."

I want to be sarcastic and point out that these are all the friends he bought by giving them jobs and buying them drinks, but I suspect Sebastián knows this already.

"Hey, well, I have to go back inside," I say.

"Maybe I can give you a ride home tonight? The car's alcohol-free."

"I'm going to have to ask my father," I say. "But be prepared for a no."

The night winds down after nine o'clock and at that point Yolanda suggests that I take off.

"Your boyfriend's still parked outside," she says. "I've seen him there during my last two cigarette breaks."

In order to keep it somewhat honest, I let Mr. Gutiérrez know about the conversation I just had with Sebastián, and that he has offered to take both me and Lib home. My father hesitates, but because Mr. Sandoval is in such a cheery and generous mood, he agrees, though with the strong warning that if anything goes wrong, that's the end of that friendship. Oh, and I have to get dropped off first. I agree to that condition as well, though the teenage horn-dog in me has no intention of following through.

Before Lib closes the market, I let him know that he'll be doing me a great favor if he lets Sebastián drive us home tonight, and since he's excited about riding in a Saab convertible, Lib calls his parents immediately to let them know he's already got a ride.

"How thrilling," Lib keeps repeating. "And don't worry. I live in the poor part of town, but the car thieves in the area will all assume this car's already been stolen when you drive into the neighborhood."

"Nice one, Lib," I say. Sebastián's eyes widen, but he drives on anyway.

"Put some music on, I want to hear how it sounds back here," Lib says as soon as we get on the main avenue. Sebastián complies.

After a few blocks on the road, Lib makes another request: "I love the Black Eyed Peas! A little less bass."

"Lib!" I say.

"That's all right," Sebastián says, and turn a knob on the panel. "Is that better, Lib?"

"Perfect. Are you going to bring the top down?"

I roll my eyes. "Anyway," I say, twisting my head around to face Lib. "How was the first night on the job?"

Lib sways his shoulders. "*Fabulous!* I even had an offer for Frida, so I'm thinking I might make some more and bring them in, you know, as a sale on the side."

"Like on consignment?" Sebastián asks.

"Maybe," Lib says. "I mean, they *are* my creations."

"But it's not your store, Lib, be careful with that," I say. "Ask Mr. Gutiérrez about it."

Lib now begins to bob his head. "Don't worry, I will. Hey, can you raise the volume when you get into my hood? Otherwise we won't be able to hear the music since everyone else will be blaring their tunes to the max."

"Sure," Sebastián says.

Indeed, Lib's neighborhood is having its own party times, and we blend right in. At Lib's insistence, we drive around his block once so that he can wave at people he knows from the backseat. More than a few of his neighbors comment on the car.

"I work at Las Cazuelas now!" he yells out each time. "Come by and I'll get you a discount!"

Finally, we pull over at his house, where Mr. and Mrs. García come out to greet us and to congratulate Lib on his first night of employment.

"They're so supportive, it's scary," I say as soon as we say our goodbyes and hit the road.

"To come from a home that's *not* broken," Sebastián says. "How's that for something different."

"It happens," I say.

We don't exchange many words on the way to my house. We're both tired. I've been standing all night and he's been sitting in the car the whole time, waiting for me to clock out. It's actually anticlimactic when we pull into the driveway to say goodnight. It's another moment of déjà vu for me. Except this time it's Sebastián and not Isaac. I suppose I need to stop comparing them since they're two very different people. But then again, they're both tall and good-looking guys I have the hots for. It's hard not to think of one when I think of the other.

"What's in your head right now?" Sebastián asks.

I giggle. "Something naughty."

"Really?"

"Well, not that naughty," I say.

He reaches over to hold my hand. Now there's something Isaac and I didn't really do. And then when he pulls my hand on his crotch, I get all flustered.

"Uh," I say. "Look, Sebastián, it's not that I don't want to get a little more physical with you. I mean, I get physical with myself like that all the time, but I'm not really ready to take that step with anyone else."

He lets go of my hand. "So you *are* a virgin," he says. "Wow, that just makes it sexier." He leans over to put his mouth on my neck. I push him away.

"Hey, you're not listening," I say. "I think it's cool that you like me. I like you too, but this isn't something I just want to jump into."

"Hmm," he says. "Even real girls are easier than you."

"You've slept with girls?"

"I used to. Until I figured out I liked boys better. But you're the first one that's not putting out."

"Putting out?" I say.

"Man, what's your game?" Sebastián says, exasperated. "Are you some kind of prude or something? We're the class of 2011. Sex is no big deal anymore."

"I'm not even going to bother arguing about this," I say, and I get out of the car.

"What? Are you kidding me? You're going to walk out on me again?"

"Not really, I'm just saying good night," I say and start walking away, trying to hide the lump in my pants. I suppose I could just give in, but not like this, in the driveway of my family's house! That's just a bit too vulgar for my taste. Maybe I'm expecting too much, like romance.

I look back. Sebastián sits in his car watching me. He's expecting me to change my mind, to turn around, rush back into the car and "put out." So I go for the kill-joy.

"Go home and take a cold shower, Sebastián," I say.

He drives off, dissatisfied, I'm sure. And I walk into my room to finish what he started, to let my imagination do for me what I wouldn't do for Sebastián.

Advice from Girls

Saturdays are going to get lonesome for me if they continue like this: Trini's still cocooned inside her Glamorous Grotto, Sebastián and I are still not allowed to visit outside of school days, and Lib is working a full shift at the Mexican curio market. And since Mickey has already signed me up to Maddy's baby shower planning committee, I tag along to the Lame View Mall, where the other committee members, Sandra and Janet, are already waiting.

Except for the small spurt of life that our presence gives the food court, the mall is pretty much dead. Janet is a Filipina with long black hair. She's a true giggler—anything will get her going on a laughing fit. Sandra is a Chicana with short curly hair. She's a self-professed militant, the president of the community college Chicano Power chapter and Mickey's friend since elementary school. All three of them will be transferring to UC Riverside in the fall, which has made their bond even tighter.

"Howdy," Janet says, waving as soon as she sees us. She giggles.

"Dude," Sandra says, "the Hot Dog Factory closed. Where am I going to get my fix?"

"Hey, guys," Mickey says. "No hot dogs this week, huh? That sucks."

I think it's amusing that they refer to each other as guys while the gay boys and I refer to ourselves as girls.

Mickey looks around, frowning. "Yep," she finally assesses. "We're going to have to relocate our committee eventually. This place is gone. Oh, but check out the new security guard."

All eyes turn on a stick figure in a cop uniform. It's strange not to see Celie patrolling the mall after all these years. Her absence itself makes this place look dramatically different. And of course, the ghost of Tony Sánchez still haunts me. I look out to the place where he shot himself. My mind goes numb for a second.

"I think he's cute," Janet offers. "I'd have to fatten him up first, though. Feed him adobo and lumpia every night."

"He looks kind of wimpy to me," says Sandra. "What's up with that funny walk?"

Mickey chimes in: "Maybe it's like an old football injury or something."

"Football?" Sandra says. "Him? Dodgeball perhaps, but no way he played football. Unless he stood in for goal post." She raises both arms for effect.

I clear my throat through their laughter. "Hello, little brother in the house."

Mickey leans over to hug me. "Isn't he precious?" she says.

Great, I'm five years old again.

I don't contribute much to the discussion since it's all about the parceling out of tasks and expenses. Las Cazuelas will be providing the buffet at Mr. Gutiérrez's expense (thank you, Papi!), Janet will do the invitations since she knows calligraphy, Sandra will be supplying the materials for the party games like diaper-changing while blindfolded and racing to see who can suck apple juice out of a baby bottle the fastest (what fun!), and Mickey will coordinate the gift-giving so that there aren't too many duplicate presents (because how many pacifiers does a baby need?).

"You, Maui," Mickey says, finally turning her attention to me. "You can bring Trini and Lib along to help you."

"Do what?" I say, knowing full well that I'm getting stuck with the grunt work.

"Set-up and clean-up," she says.

I groan. "You're kidding me?"

"Papi's providing the food, but he's not paying anyone to work for the party," she explains. "And since you and Lib work there already, I think it's perfect."

"Excuse me," I say. "Lib works at the Mexican curio market and I host. That's different than wiping beans off the tables."

"Even better, Maui," Sandra says. "It gives you a chance to learn about the exhausting labor Mexicans have to contend with in most parts of the country, including here in the Caliente Valley."

"Oh, Sandra," Janet says, giggling. "Don't worry him about those things. He's still in high school."

"All the more reason he needs to know the truth. Before he's fed any more lies," Sandra says. She then turns to me: "Look around you, Maui. This recession has tons of invisible victims: the undocumented laborers, the farmworkers, the dishwashers and busboys at Las Cazuelas. And I know that ever since Sandoval Construction arrived here it's been hailed as the Second Coming, but he's refusing to employ the day laborers or even to allow a union contract. Without the power of collective bargaining, what's to become of us when one company monopolizes the industry?"

It's refreshing but also frightening to hear someone speak negatively of Mr. Sandoval for once. I'm not sure what to do with that information.

Mickey steps in, apologetically. "Sandra, really," she says. "You know my father treats every employee with dignity."

"Your father is one person," Sandra says. "Mr. Benson is another."

"Mr. Benson can be generous," Mickey counters.

Sandra looks at her through the corner of her eye: "I'm sure he can."

Janet giggles, "Isn't this fun, Maui? Okay, guys, relax. We're here to talk baby showers, remember? But it looks to me like some of us need happy showers. Help me douse them with a group hug, Maui."

It's cheesy and, for me, awkward because I have no idea about this group's history or dynamics, but it seems to do the trick at the moment, and Sandra backs off with her protest rally. Not even Lib during his political phase got this intense. Mickey takes it all in stride and moves on.

"Walter agreed to provide the cake," Mickey says. "And he'll bring it toward the end of the party since he can't be there because of his shift at his new job at the construction site."

I look over at Sandra, who doesn't react.

Mickey continues: "As for the party favors, I decided on bibs. Mrs. García, bless her heart, has volunteered to sew on a patch on each one to commemorate the occasion."

"What's on the patch?" I ask.

"The date and Maddy's name, as well as the baby's name," Mickey replies.

Janet giggles. "How fun! They already picked a name. Boy or girl?"

"They want it to be a surprise," Mickey says. "So the name's gender-neutral: Robbie. Robbie Simmons-Johnson."

"I like it," Janet says, though I suspect there's very little she doesn't like, except conflict.

"I'll say one thing about Walter," Sandra says. "At least he didn't leave Maddy to suffer the pregnancy alone. I'm still in disbelief that he even wanted to marry her."

"He's of a different breed, that's for certain," Mickey says. And then she remembers I'm in the group. "Maybe you should plug your ears, Maui."

"Oh, come on!" Sandra protests. "Now he can't hear about these things either? I'm sure he's not as innocent as he looks, Mickey. You're infantilizing him."

Janet interrupts, "Now, Sandra, this is Mickey's baby brother, I'm sure she knows him better than we do."

But before Mickey has a chance to gloat I speak up.

"I can speak for myself, guys," I say. "Believe me, I know all about the exploitation of cheap labor, and about the birds and the bees, and how in our economically-depressed little town we have more high school dropouts and teenage pregnancies than college-bound students. I know that most of us never make it out of here, either because we get swallowed up in the low expectations society has imposed on us, or because we can't overcome our private traumas. I lost one friend because he became a teenage runaway and I have another friend who's hiding out because he doesn't know what to do about her abusive father. And just a few feet away is where I lost a friend who never had a chance to be himself because besides being poor, the Caliente Valley's also homophobic and riddled with gangs. I don't need any more preparation for life than simply walking out the front door! But if you really want to help, then maybe you can answer me this: when do you know the time is right to finally have sex with a guy?"

"All righty, then," Mickey says. "I guess the kid stays."

After a brief silence, Sandra gets the ball rolling: "Well, I'm the cynic in the group, so I can tell you this: if you're in love, it won't be the first time, or the last. And most likely he's going to break your heart anyway, so you might as well have a good time while you're in the moment of temporary delusion and deception."

"Now, wait a minute," Janet says. "Some people believe in intimacy with only the people they truly love. I can count in one hand how many that's been for me. And I don't regret those choices, or the choices I made when I didn't become physically involved." Then she giggles, amused by how well she handled it.

"Maybe I should plug my ears," Mickey says. She takes a deep breath. "Well, Maui. You're going to do what you're going to do no matter what. But you yourself just said that making a stupid mistake can cost you your future. You can't get pregnant, you lucky dog, but there are other dangers to watch out for. Not all of us can get as lucky as Maddy. The rest of us can't take that risk and must watch every step we take. And just because you're a guy doesn't mean that you can throw caution to the wind or that you won't have regrets. You're going to make mistakes, that's true. But why rush into them when you don't have to?"

Sandra nods. "Yeah, Mickey's right. No man is worth it."

"True," Janet agrees, and then all three of them drift off into their own memory waves.

"Thanks," I say. I appreciate that they didn't tell me what to do, but they certainly gave me plenty to think about. Big sisters are the best.

"Who is this prince charming, anyway?" Sandra asks.

Janet giggles. "Yeah, Maui. Is he cute?"

"Sebastián Sandoval," I say. "The heir of Sandoval Construction."

An eerie silence descends on the group. Smiles vanish, and they start making eye contact.

"What?" I ask.

"Nothing," Mickey says, giving Sandra and Janet the eye. "Absolutely nothing. You're a lucky boy, that's all. Right, guys?"

"Right," Sandra and Janet say, though their enthusiasm is unconvincing.

We clear the table and I notice Sandra whispering into Mickey's ear, but I can't decipher her words. Whatever secret they've got they're going to keep it from me, and suddenly I'm cast back to my role as the little brother who doesn't need to know everything. Not right away, anyway.

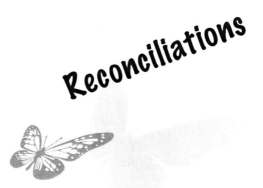

Reconciliations

Yolanda calls in sick on Sunday and I'm expecting nothing more exciting than trying to read Lib's lips from a distance, but there's at least one interesting development: After a week of silence, Trini finally emerges, looking more like a boy than before because her face is expressionless and sullen. She comes in for Sunday brunch with her parents, pushing Aunt Carmen's wheelchair in front of her.

"Mauricio," Mrs. Ramos says. "How are you? We're going to need a table with room for Aunt Carmen's chair."

"Certainly," I say. I look down at my chart. "Would you care to browse in our new Mexican curio market while the space clears? It'll be about five minutes."

"That looks like fun, doesn't it Aunt Carmen?" she says. "I'm sure Aunt Carmen will love to see some of those *rebozos*."

Mr. Ramos nods his head at me and follows Mrs. Ramos and Aunt Carmen into the market. Lib cranes his neck to look at Trini.

“Aunt Carmen’s looking better,” I say.

“She’s doing much better,” Trini says. She purses her lips. “Look, Maui, I can’t explain now, but let me just tell you that things are better at home, between my father and me.”

“Is that why you were absent from school for a week?” I ask.

“That’s another story,” Trini says. “Maybe one that I can tell you if you come to the Glamorous Grotto tonight?”

I can’t resist and smile. “Sounds like an invitation I can’t refuse. Should I tell Lib?”

“Of course. I can’t imagine a tea party without our third cup,” Trini says, snapping her fingers. She cringes and looks over her shoulder. She’s safe; Mr. Ramos didn’t catch her.

The remaining hours at work drag on, especially because I’m hosting solo, but the good thing about Sundays is that the restaurant closes early, so by four thirty that afternoon, we’re disappointing potential customers—the kitchen’s closing. The Mexican curio market closed half an hour ago, but instead of going home, Lib hangs out with me at the hostess station so that we can kill the final hour at work together. Besides, Trini promised to pick us up.

“What do you think she’s been up to, that crazy gal?” Lib says. “I bet you anything she went on a hunger strike. She certainly looked scrawnier than usual.”

“True,” I say. “Though who knows? She’s full of surprises, that’s for sure.”

“And what about you and Mr. Bootylicious? Sneak around with him lately?”

“No,” I say. “I think we’re giving this thing a break. There are so many things he needs to sort out before he throws me into the mix. It’s going to be hard, but I’m keeping my legs crossed.”

Lib pats me on the back. “Good for you, sister,” he says. “It takes a solid conviction and maybe a bit of insanity to say no to a guy like Sebastián, but who says it can’t be done?”

I grin and say, "Thanks."

"By the way," he says. "I got Mr. Benson's permission to sell my Gothic skeleton ballerinas in the market. I can only bring one at a time, though, which is fine by me because they're not that easy to make."

"Cool," I say. "How much are they going for?"

"Twenty-five bucks, wholesale," Lib says, beaming. "If I can sell one a week, that will add up to a nice piggy bank fund by the end of the summer. I've already been hearing back from colleges, have you?"

"Not yet," I say. "But now that we're on that topic—"

Lib cuts me off. "I know what you're about to say, Maui, and I'm telling you that I'm fine with going to the college we *both* get accepted to. We need to stick together! It'll be only two musketeers by then. It's important. How else are we going to survive out *there*, in that big, scary world?"

We look out through the entrance of the restaurant, at the February sky getting darker, at the car headlights burning holes through the twilight. Suddenly that side of the door looks less familiar, more uncertain, and the thought of stepping into it alone sends a shudder down my spine. But at the same time, I feel as if it's important to go into it alone, without a safety net, with no weapons but the shaky street smarts that I'm very quickly accumulating. I'll let Lib keep holding on to the fantasy a while longer. When the time comes, he too will be ready to go on by himself.

The door bursts open and it startles me.

"Ready to roll," Trini asks, Paulina Rubio's keys dangling in her hands.

"Ready." I say. When it's the three of us, no threshold can stop us.

Unfortunately, Trini's CD player broke so we have to screech our theme song for the day—Cyndi Lauper's classic "I Drove All

Night"—until we get to the Glamorous Grotto. By the time we get there I need a glass of water.

"Well, it looks cleaner, at least," Lib comments when we walk inside. Trini hasn't replaced any of the old wall décor.

"Baby steps," Trini says. "May I offer you girls some iced tea with lemon cake? Check this out!" She points at a small refrigerator in the corner.

"Moving on up," I say. "How much did this set you back?"

"Not much," she says. "We got it on layaway at K-Mart. Oh, and feast your fake eyelashes on this!"

Trini does his Vanna White display gesture as she pulls the blanket off a television set.

"Oh. My. Goddess," Lib says. "She robbed a bank!"

"Trini?" I say. "Where did you get the money for this?"

Trini sucks her teeth. "Of course, I didn't rob a bank. And, no, I didn't sell myself at some Palm Springs parking lot, either. Really, girls! Let's just say this was part of the peace agreement between my father and me."

"Explain," I say. Somehow I can't see it. First Mr. Ramos gets angry over a five-dollar magazine and then he turns around and gives Trini a brand new television? Doesn't make one lick of sense.

Trini motions to the divan. "Sit. Relax. And let me tell you a tale about how a bully like Mr. Ramos was brought to his knees. Ha, ha, ha, ha." She does that diabolical pretend laugh at the end.

As it turns out, Mr. Ramos went too far one day, to the point that Aunt Carmen rose from her bed and staggered right up to him and gave him a firm swat with the closest thing she could pick up: a glass candlestick. It didn't knock him out, but it sent a strong message, so Mrs. Ramos followed it up by picking up a second candlestick and giving Mr. Ramos a swat in the groin that made him take notice.

Trini, who had been cowering in the corner of the room under the threat of Mr. Ramos' hand, watched incredulously as Mr. Ramos begged for forgiveness.

"I was waiting for him to get his revenge," Trini says. "So I locked myself in here, not even daring to go to school. And they left me alone the whole time, though things were changing over there as well. It turns out my father applied for an opening at one of the construction sites and got the job. So he's happier now that he makes more money. Plus, are you ready for this?"

Lib and I nod our heads.

"Mami's preggers!" Trini says. "I'm not going to be an only child anymore!"

"All that at once," I say. "No wonder he crumbled."

"Well, congrats, Trini," Lib says. "Now you and Celie and Mickey can form like the Big Sister Club or something. How fabulous!"

"Isn't it? Me, a big sister!"

"So, then why the mini-fridge and the TV?" I ask.

"Oh, peace tokens, I think," Trini says. "Since they'll be converting my bedroom into the nursery, eventually. I mean, when that baby starts crying at night, only two of us won't be able to hear it: Aunt Carmen, who's deaf, and me, because I'll be out here. In my new home."

Lib and I look at each other. Okay, first they force all of her stuff into the outdoor closet, and now they invite her to live in it full time. Something's not right about this.

"Trini." I say. "Are you okay with this?"

"Sure," she says, her lips trembling this time around. "I mean, why should I get in the way of my parents starting all over again, and maybe getting it right this time? Maybe this kid will be normal, how's that for a blessing?"

When the tears come, it's hard not to cry along with her.

Mariposa Gown

"Oh, let's stop this, you two," Trini says. "I'm not in this for the Oscar nomination. Damn, I don't even have any eye makeup on to wipe clean. Just boring, transparent tears not even worth the trouble. Let's change the subject, shall we?"

"Well," Lib says, stammering. "We did get a chance to talk to Mr. Beasley about the prom."

"You did? And what did he say? Did his comb-over flip?"

That image sets off the laughs. "Yes," I say. "He's convinced we're going to ruin all the straight kids' night if we have two males run for King and Queen."

"How silly," Trini says. "That happens every four years in this country, except that we call them President and Vice-President."

"You should have been there to tell him that one," Lib says.

"And have you started cooking up the gown of gowns, Trini?" I say. "I can see you in blue chiffon, maybe something feathery."

"Stop it, you're going to make me lady-faint," Trini says. "This is going to be the best night ever. It'll certainly be payback for the time I ran for Homecoming Queen and almost got killed."

My heart skips a beat. That's right, I had almost forgotten. The last time Trini tried something like this it put her in danger. I look at Lib for support and he seems to be thinking the same thing.

"You know, Trini," he says. "You don't have to go through with this if you don't want to. What if your father finds out?"

"Pshaw, ladies," Trini says. "I *want* to do this. I *need* to do this. How else will I have my big moment? You two are going away to college, Sebastián is off to who knows where, and I want to give you all a parting gift that you'll never forget."

"No, Trini, really," I say. "You can say no."

"And I can also say yes, can't I?" She gets up to consider herself in the mirror. "It'll be a show-stopper all right. Trinidad Ramos, Queen of the Prom."

An uneasy feeling comes over me. But at the very least, we're back together again, the Fierce Trio, and no harm can come to us as long as we've got each other.

PART TWO

May Madness, June Joy

Senioritis

If I could collapse the months of March and April into a sandwich, it wouldn't be very appetizing. It would still be a meal, of course, but it would be an ordinary one—the familiar food groups in their usual positions on the cafeteria tray.

During this time, Lib's orders for his Gothic ballerinas kept him busy and every time someone bought one of his works of art, no sooner was the client out of the market that he'd ring it up in his imaginary cash register, *Ka-ching!* It got annoying after a while, but I just smiled and sometimes applauded him from the hostess station.

Trini worked tirelessly on stitching the sequins on her prom dress at the Glamorous Grotto and promised a full unveiling soon. Mr. Ramos has kept his temper on the down-low, and I've noticed that Trini has quietly crept back into her blouses—the more conservative ones, anyway.

As for me, I only saw Sebastián in school, and on occasion at Las Cazuelas, when he was called upon to pick up his tipsy father on a Friday night. Okay, that's not really true. Once in a blue moon I'd let him take me to Smooching Summit, where we indeed smooched and nothing else, which infuriated Sebastián each time. I mean, think about it: why would I want my first sexual experience to be with a guy who thinks sex is not a big deal? I'd just be setting myself for unnecessary heartache.

The only event worth writing home about was Maddy's baby shower at the restaurant, which was kind of fun in a domestic kind of way. Snake made his proud papa entrance with the cake at the right moment, and Mickey, Sandra and Janet beamed into the evening because the festivities ran their course without a single snag. Sheriff Johnson stopped by and we did that nod-from-a-distance thing, but as far as I know we've let bygones be bygones.

Spring Break came and went, and all Lib and I got was an extended work week at Las Cazuelas. For Sebastián, probably the only kid in the school who could afford it, it was a chance to get away from the Caliente Valley finally. He spent a week in Acapulco with marble-bag-clad Spring Breakers from all over the country, and then the weekend before classes started he flew to New York City. He brought the Mariposa Club members snow globes with a miniature Empire State Building inside.

By this time, Lib and I received acceptances or rejections from the colleges we applied to. And though we were all gung-ho about attending a big city university at first, reality set in with the details of the expense. Even with that scholarship Lib received from the LGBT coalition it didn't seem like he had enough. So our choices were considerably limited. And even though I begged Lib to take out of his head this idea that we *had* to attend the same school, he wouldn't budge. And in the end, we decided that we would attend UC Riverside, just an hour away. This thrilled Lib's parents, who weren't looking forward to letting go of their son. Even Mickey, who was transferring to the same college in the fall as a junior, thought it was a good idea, that way all five of us (Lib, Sandra, Janet, Mickey and I) could ride down to the valley together to visit our families. Though it was made clear from the start that Mickey and I would not be living together. Amen to that.

At this point in the program, every high school senior is on automatic mode. It's almost anti-climactic to come to class since we're more invested in daydreaming as we count down the days to graduation. Everything related to school work from this moment forward is done half-assed. The only thing to look forward to before graduation is Senior Prom, and though Boozely hasn't mentioned anything about the Mariposa Club's plans to nominate Trini for Prom Queen, I've caught him giving us the combed-over eagle eye from a distance as we congregate at the Queer Planter.

The only other stirring in the horizon is Cinco de Mayo, which is only a few days away, and Mr. Benson and Mr. Gutiérrez have a whole weekend of activities planned. I'm in charge of shuttling around the usual suspects at any Mexican festivity: the ballet folklórico, the mariachi band, and the puppeteer who's coming in a few times to entertain the children. They cleared out a space for a performing stage, which shrinks the dining space down a bit since the boss didn't want to lose any tables. Yolanda scoffed at that wise decision: "Great, now we're going to have to smear our bodies against each other just to get through!"

Otherwise, the dust has settled over the Caliente Valley. Famous last words, I know, but let me cling on to them for a while longer, before the desert dust storms begin.

On the last evening of April, Mickey and I are sitting in front of the television, only partly engaged since she's doing her nails while she's got the phone on her ear and I've taken the night off from hosting because Yolanda owes me a day, so I'm absent-mindedly getting through the final chapters of *East of Eden*. I'm still rolling my eyes at why we needed parental consent forms to read this book when regular family-hour TV programming is more scandalous than this. Besides, it takes a lot of word mining to get through the grittier scenes of the novel. I'm at the part of the book when Caleb decides to stab his brother in the heart by taking him to visit their mother, who's now the colorful town prostitute, when Papi bursts through the door.

"You're home early," I say. "Everything okay?"

My father glances at me for a moment, though he seems more interested in Mickey. "Yeah, sure," he says. "I had to come pick up some paperwork I left behind. Has your sister been on the phone long?"

"For hours," I say. "Why? Did you try to call?"

"Repeatedly," he says.

I elbow Mickey. "Get off the phone, nerd. Papi wants to talk to you."

"Hey!" Mickey complains. When she notices the stern look on Papi's face, she cuts short her conversation. "What's the matter, Papi?"

When my father hesitates like that, it's big. I put the book down. This is going to get good.

Papi finally spits it out. "Mickey, what do you know about the protests planned for International Workers' Day?"

Now Mickey hesitates, which means she knows all about it and hadn't counted on fessing up while doing her nails on the couch.

"Uhm, well," she stammers. "It's really Sandra's group from the community college. I'm not really part of it but I'm lending my support."

"What's going on?" I ask.

"Well, Maui," Papi says. "You know that I believe in organizing for a good cause, and that the expression of political beliefs is a right that I would never deny either one of you, but I'm not feeling this one. This group that Sandra's part of has riled up the Mexican workers at the restaurant. They're walking out on the job tomorrow and rallying in front of the offices of Sandoval Construction."

"What?" I sit up. "But tomorrow we kick off the Cinco de Mayo celebrations! It's going to be chaos without them!"

"Oh, it was quite a scene. Sandra stormed into the restaurant, wearing her Che Guevara beret, and with an entourage of Chicanos passing out literature to our customers. It was all very disruptive."

"Oh, man," I say. "My one night off and I miss all the excitement."

Mickey's jaw drops. "Papi, you're not blaming *me* for this, are you? I wasn't part of it."

Papi runs his hand though his receding hairline. "I know, I know, but I recognized Sandra, and when I asked them to leave they wouldn't budge. They came in because they knew Mr. Sandoval was having dinner there. Sandra gave this militant speech about oppressing the day laborers. And then they marched out before the police arrived."

"I didn't know they were going to do *that*," Mickey says.

"But you *did* know they were planning this protest tomorrow?" Papi asks.

Mickey nods her head.

My father looks conflicted, but there's nothing else he can do, so he goes back to his room to pick up the paperwork he needed, and then he leaves the house again. The door doesn't slam shut subtly.

At least now the knowing glances that passed between Mickey and Sandra back at the mall when I told them I was crushing on Sebastián make sense.

"You know, Mickey," I say. "I like Sandra and all but don't you think it's kind of rude to use Las Cazuelas to throw a baby shower for Maddy one day and then turn right back around and SWAT team the place to make a political statement?"

"Maui, hush! I said I didn't know they were going to do that. I guess they knew it would be a conflict of interest for me."

"And what about for her?" I say. "She knows Papi. Shit, she's been coming over here for years. She even knew Mami!"

"All right, Maui, I got it!" She bites on her lips. "Sandra's certainly become more passionate about this whole Chicano Power thing. It's like she has something to prove before she leaves the community college. Why can't she just move on without having to go out with some big bang?"

A shadow of recognition falls over me. Isn't that something? I guess the Mariposa Club is not the only organization trying to change its world.

Mickey picks up the phone and dials. "She's not picking up. She's probably out at headquarters."

"Headquarters?" I say. "What organization did you say she belonged to—the KGB?"

Mickey rubs her hand over her forehead. "Oh, my God. Listen, Maui, can you drive me over to the college grounds? I'm too upset."

I drop John Steinbeck on the floor. "Gladly!" I say.

It's not that I finally have a chance to sit behind the wheel of Mickey's car instead of Papi's steamboat Cadillac that excites me since driving through the streets of Caliente is no Indy 500 experience, but I'm dying to find out what all of the fuss is about. Within half an hour we're parking in front of an old beat up shack that passes for the community college radio station. Mickey leads the way, her nails ruined since she put her jacket on before the polish dried. I can barely keep up.

The inside of the radio station is just as unimpressive as the outside. Since they crammed both WKOD and Chicano Power into one room, the place looks just the opposite of the Glamorous Grotto: crowded, disorganized and smelly. They smoke all kinds of things in here, if you catch my drift.

"Phew!" I say. "They should really open a window."

Though it looks like having more than five bodies in here at once is a fire code violation, there are at least fifteen college kids scattered over anything they can lean or sit on. Behind a glass window, a fat guy with a beard wears headphones and spins the records. Sandra sits on a desk chair.

"Mickey," Sandra says. "What a surprise. I guess you heard."

Mickey starts to cry and this gets everyone's attention, including the sleepy dude in the corner who looks like he's only awake five minutes a day. "I can't believe you, Sandra," she says. "You humiliated my father in public. He's been nothing but good to you all these years!"

Sandra looks away. "Some things are bigger than friendly relationships. May first: International Workers' Day. The rights of every laborer to earn a fair and honest living. That's what matters."

"Sandra!" Mickey yells. "This is *me* you're talking to, don't give me your pamphlet propaganda."

Sandra sighs. She gets up and takes Mickey outside, I want to follow but one of the Chicano Power comrades stops me. "It's between the two comrades," he says. I feel as if I'm expected to salute.

The sleepy dude offers me Sandra's seat. "It might take a while," he says.

I sit down and put my hands on my lap. At first everyone looks at me but eventually they lose interest and go back to their conversations. Only the sleepy dude takes it upon himself to keep me entertained.

"So you're Maui, Mickey's little bro?" he asks.

I nod.

"Yeah, I know you. You work with my cousin at Las Cazuelas. Yolanda."

"Small world," I say, which isn't really saying much because we live in such a small town. "Was she happy about you paratrooping the restaurant tonight?"

"Paratrooping?" Sleepy Dude chuckles and looks around him but no one's listening. "Nah, little bro, we were just getting the message out. I hope you'll join us tomorrow when we rally in front of Sandoval Construction."

My ears perk up. I suppose that this is my only chance to get any information, so I decide to milk the opportunity. Sleepy Dude's not a bad looking guy at all, except that he needs a haircut and a shave. The scruffy look ages him.

"I have to work tomorrow," I say.

"Yeah, but tomorrow every Mexican worker's going to walk out on the job. You've got to show solidarity, little bro."

"I should not work to show how much I value work? Makes no sense to me. And why are you targeting Mr. Sandoval, anyway. He's given many people employment."

"That may be true, little bro, but at the expense of what?" Sleepy Dude says, though he's now shifted into his preacher mode. I expect him to break out into song any minute. "No union contracts, poor health insurance plans, a weak worker's compensation deal. It's all in here."

He hands me a pamphlet that reads: ***Sandoval Destruction!***

Sleepy Dude goes on: "Not to mention the refusal of jobs to our brothers from the south, the day laborers. He may look like a savior from the outside, but from the inside he's just another money-grubbing, worker-exploiting capitalist."

I fold the pamphlet and tuck it into the palm of my hand. Geez, and Mr. Sandoval seemed like such a nice person.

"Quit scaring the kid, Mando," a young woman wearing a Zapatista shirt comes to my rescue.

"Just educating the little bro, that's all," he says, and backs off.

"Hey," she says, kneeling down beside me.

"Hey," I say.

"You like music? You want DJ Lobo there to play one of your favorite tunes?" she asks. "What do you like? Ozomatli?"

Because I'm in a melancholy mood all of a sudden, I blurt out: "Lila Downs."

A group cheer follows. "Yeah, you see? Little bro knows where it's at," Sleepy Dude says.

The young woman in the Zapatista shirt presses a button on the console and relays my request. DJ Lobo gives her the thumbs up.

As Sandra and Mickey make peace outside, I sit inside the crowded radio station, listening to Lila Downs. This is definitely a scene I had not anticipated. I can imagine Lib fitting into a group like this, but not me. Maybe. I don't know. I'm just trying to get through the final months of high school. But then I realize, after June that's not going to be an excuse anymore. I can't just whip that handy phrase around for much longer. I guess this is what growing up is all about—thinking seriously about standing on my own two feet.

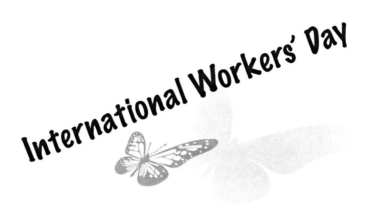

International Workers' Day

Times are tough, and not everybody at Las Cazuelas participates in the walk-out, although those who do are guaranteed that they won't get fired because it says in the pamphlet Mando gave me at the radio station last night that any employer dismissing an employee over this planned civil protest will be duly slapped with an ACLU lawsuit and daily protests. That's certainly not the kind of publicity Mr. Benson wants at his restaurant, so he walks around sneering and growling at the rest of us.

"That's gratitude for you," Yolanda says. "He just told me he was limiting my cigarette breaks."

"I guess you can think of it as saving minutes on your cell," I say. She's not amused.

"Ka-ching!" Lib calls out. I roll my eyes.

"Give me a sec," I tell Yolanda, and then I walk over to the curio market.

"Hey, Lib. Drama central, huh?"

"No kidding," Lib says. "I could hear Sandra from all the way back here last night. Poor Mr. Sandoval looked like he would've strangled her if he hadn't been on his fourth pitcher of margaritas."

"Maybe I should call Sebastián," I say.

"And how's Mickey doing? I'm sure she's not a happy camper."

I sigh. "We drove over to confront Sandra last night, but I'm not sure where it ended. She was so upset she cried all the way home."

"Sucks," Lib says. "Well, Trini said she was joining the counter-demonstration."

"Counter-demonstration? What are you talking about?"

Lib shakes his head. "Hello! You didn't think someone like Mr. Sandoval was just going to take it lying down, did you? He organized his employees to stage a rally to counter the accusations of this other group. Mr. Ramos will be there, Trini, even Maddy and Snake."

"And here we are missing all the action!" I say. Suddenly I turn to lib: "And why aren't *you* there, Mr. Politics?"

"Some things are bigger than politics," Lib says. "My loyalty's to your father, who gave me a job I really needed. Since the restaurant's short-staffed, I'm joining the kitchen brigade in the evening. As are you."

"I am?" I say.

As if on cue, my father comes up behind me. "Oh, Maui, there you are. Listen, do me a huge favor tonight and help out in the kitchen with Lib. We're a little understaffed today, as you know, so we need all hands on deck." He walks away before I have a chance to respond.

"Told you," Lib says.

"Well, I guess I was bound to end up there eventually," I respond.

"Hey, Maui," Yolanda says. "The puppet guy is here. Can you show him to the back room?"

I greet Señor Pepe the puppeteer with a large trunk on a dolly. Somehow we squeeze through the narrow walking spaces and make it to the employees' locker room. He's sweating profusely, but his handlebar mustache wears the exertion well.

"This looks exciting," I say when he opens the trunk, which is a chaos of wooden puppets, cross-shaped control bars and wound-up strings. "Cool puppets," I add.

"Marionettes," Señor Pepe counters. Testy old guy.

"Cool marionettes," I say.

Though it appears to bother him, I stick around for a few minutes to watch him pull out a few of his marionettes—or rather, miniature stereotypes of Mexican people. There's a pretty señorita with large thick eyelashes and her cohort, a potbellied Mexican who's probably quite comfortable sleeping beneath a cactus. Oh, brother. If Chicano Power could see this, they'd want to cut the strings and set these poor underpaid and overworked performers free.

"I'm sure the kids will *love* this," I say, though Señor Pepe doesn't really want to hear it. I decide to quit while I'm ahead and leave the cranky puppeteer alone. He's got a roomful of antsy children to contend with in about an hour.

Back at the hostess station, I learn that the paperwork my father came to pick up was some old contact information for former employees. A few of them were persuaded to come for the weekend for twice the pay. None of the customers even notice all the damage control behind the scenes as Mr. Benson and Mr. Gutiérrez struggle to pull the evening together without any complications. The acts all fall behind schedule but that wasn't their problem: the mariachi van broke down just outside of town and Yolanda had to volunteer her truck for an emergency pick-up. Their entrance wasn't as graceful, but they made it eventually.

The Mexican curio market closed down even sooner than planned and I left my station immediately after to help move things along in the kitchen. The large dishwashers were easy to operate, but first we had to scrape or rinse the beans and cheese off the plates, which was disgusting.

"This is gross," Lib says, stating the obvious. But when I look it turns out that someone left an item on the plate that probably wasn't there in the first place.

"What is that? Someone's teeth?" I say.

"Dentures of some kind," Lib says. He uses a fork to fish them out and holds them up. "Anybody lose their taco chompers?" he announces, biting into the air.

The other kitchen workers burst out into laughter. It's the only moment of levity we will have for the rest of the evening.

We break a sweat in front of the hot running water and by the end I feel like I'm wiping perspiration off the clean plates. But somehow we make it to closing time.

"I need to borrow some strings from Señor Pepe," Lib says. "I can't move my own arms."

"Don't be such a wimp, Lib, a little exercise won't hurt," I say, though I'm really inclined to agree with him.

We sit in the waiting area at the entrance for Mickey to come by to drive us home. It's going to be a long night at Las Cazuelas for Mr. Gutiérrez.

"Can you believe we have to be here tomorrow at ten?" I say. "Kill me now."

"I wonder how it went with Trini and them," Lib wonders aloud.

We get our answer when Mickey arrives and she fills us in on the way home. It turns out that Sheriff Johnson put a stop to all of it—the demonstrators, the counter-demonstrators—because they were all congregating without official permission. This only intensified the situation so he arrested the ringleaders: Sandra and Mr. Ramos.

"Are you kidding me?" I say, shocked. "It was Mr. Sandoval who organized the counter-demonstration. Why did they arrest Mr. Ramos?"

Mickey scoffs. "You didn't really think Mr. Sandoval was going to show up with a picket sign, did you? He had his puppets. Mr. Ramos was the loudest, most intimidating of the bunch, so he was assigned to lead."

"Well, this will put him in Mr. Sandoval's good graces, that's for sure," Lib says.

"What about Sandra?" I say.

"I think she reveled in the arrest," Mickey says. "She earned her stripes all right."

"I'll have to call Trini when I get home," I say.

"Crazy," Lib says. "Crazy days in the Caliente Valley. I all but forgot about the prom."

"Oh, the prom," Mickey says, swept off into some euphoric memory. "You're all going? And who are your dates?"

Lib and I look at each other.

"That's a story for another time, sis," I say.

I can't say I'm too distraught over Trini's father behind bars, though he's locked up for the wrong reason. Hopefully Mr. Sandoval will slip him a bonus through the jail bars, that way Mr. Ramos won't get home all pissed off and take it out on Trini.

We drop Lib off and then get home soon after. I rush to the phone as soon I walk in the house.

"Hello," a shaky voice answers. It's Trini.

"Trini, are you okay?" I ask. "Are you hurt?"

"No, nothing like that. We're just a little upset that's all. My mother won't stop crying."

I want to say, *Okay, and what's your excuse?* But I hold my tongue.

"Just the thought of my poor father spending the night in jail breaks my heart," Trini says.

"He'll survive. Besides, Sandra's in there keeping him company."

"Sandra was released," Trini explains. "But my father's facing assault charges."

"Assault?"

"Yes," Trini says. "He didn't go into the squad car as peacefully as Sandra did. He struck one of the officers."

Somehow it fits his behavioral pattern, I want to say. But again, I keep it to myself.

"I don't think he'll lose his job or anything," I say to offer some comfort. "I mean, it was Mr. Sandoval's idea for him to be out there counter-demonstrating."

"Maybe. I have to go now, Maui. Mami needs me."

I hang up. I guess a child's love in unconditional. I can understand how I can love a father like Papi, but to love a father like Mr. Ramos? I mention this to Mickey.

"Maui," she says. "That's a terrible thing to say. Trini loves his father. You don't know a person unless you've walked in his shoes."

It sounds all wrong. It's *her father, her shoes.* Even the word *love.* But my wise older sister is right. I *don't* know. This is just another one of those intangibles a mariposa can't wrap her brain around.

Cinco de Mayo

Cinco de Mayo is not really celebrated on May fifth—not at Las Cazuelas anyway, since Cinco de Mayo falls on a weekday and Mr. Benson wants to party on the weekend when the droves of revelers are likely to come in. So, like everything else around here, we simply make do and call Sunday Cinco de Mayo since Saturday was the kick-off. It's the spirit of the holiday that counts, not the actual calendar day.

Mr. Gutiérrez brings back the mariachi band, whose members are looking tired and dehydrated, and the fat trumpet player in particular should be put out of his misery. But they're good sports and give a lively performance for the brunch crowd. Señor Pepe, I discovered, hides his cantankerous personality behind his marionettes, who have perpetual smiles carved into their heads. The only moment of true tension that morning is when one of the kids squatting in the front shoots a spit wad at one of the marionettes that passes near him. In retaliation, the marionette walks back and kicks the kid on the knee, which probably didn't hurt, but the shock of the response sends the kid crying to his mother. The kid's father has a sense of humor about the whole thing but the mother's inconsolable. Mr. Gutiérrez offers the brat a complimentary sundae, but he shoots me a look from afar that says, *Next year, no Pepe.*

The rest of the day drags on without incident, but we're staying open later than usual, so there's more room for error, which comes in the shape of Mr. Sandoval, who decides to hijack Cinco de Mayo by throwing a party for his counter-demonstrators. It must be particularly awkward for the Mexican workers who were demonstrating against Sandoval Construction in the first place, but no one makes a big deal about it. That was *so* yesterday.

Mr. Benson is more than happy to oblige his number one customer, so he has the staff set up a few tables on top of the performing stage. Mr. Sandoval, apparently, has a few guests of honor: the Ramos family.

When Mr. Ramos and Trini walk in wearing almost identical suits and matching blue ties, I nearly fall back on my ass.

"Good evening, Mr. Ramos, Mrs. Ramos. Trini," I say, though if we weren't in mixed company I'd probably call her Young Mistress Trini or something.

"Mauricio." Mr. Ramos' fancy wear gives his demeanor an air of formality that seems out of place.

"Aunt Carmen's not joining you tonight?" I ask.

Mrs. Ramos leans in closely. "She's feeling a little under the weather. Thank you for asking."

When I look at Trini she winks at me and flutters her eyelashes. Yep. She's in drag.

I walk the Ramos family to the table on the stage and Mrs. Ramos blushes with surprise, though Mr. Ramos feels quite at home being the center of attention. As does Trini. They're eventually joined by Mr. Sandoval and his handsomely coiffed stud of a son Sebastián. It's obvious from afar that Trini's thrilled Sebastián takes a seat right next to her—the King and Queen indeed.

Lib walks over from the curio market to elbow me. "Well, that's a *fine* how do you do. We're out here hoofing it on the grubby cafeteria floor while Prom Princess over there plays footsie with Prince Charming. Life sucks."

It suddenly dawns on me that this is an echo of things to come. We have always assumed Trini would be nominated Prom Queen, but we haven't really named the potential Prom King. I do believe Sebastián just nominated himself. I'll have to run it by him though.

"Isn't he dashing?" Yolanda says, all gooey-eyed.

I know she's referring to Mr. Sandoval, who looks like he's running for mayor in his expensive suit and million-dollar smile, but I pretend she's talking about Sebastián, so glorious on his pedestal. "He sure is."

The mariachi band comes out and starts to blare out a festive tune. Since the stage is occupied, they stand between tables, to the dismay of the servers and busboys, who have to maneuver around them while balancing full trays.

Mr. Benson and Mr. Gutiérrez climb onto the stage and take their seats, giving the gathering further importance. They too are freshly groomed. Papi looks happy, which makes me happy.

After the band finishes playing and the applause dies down, Mr. Benson stands up to welcome the special guests. He thanks Mr. Sandoval for making Las Cazuelas his second home. There's a general group eye roll from the staff. The flattery and yadda yadda yadda goes on for a little too long, but eventually, Mr. Sandoval rises to a flurry of stomping and cheering. He bows and then takes his turn.

"Thank you, friends. Gracias, amigos," he says. It's going to be one of those *We Are Familia* speeches.

"Today we demonstrated that we can stand together and overcome racial and class divisions..."

Since I'm not part of the hurrah community my interest fades, particularly because I don't recall Mr. Sandoval standing in the front lines, getting arrested. But maybe that's just me.

Mr. Sandoval goes on: "There is one man in particular I would like for us to acknowledge and celebrate tonight, since it was he who took the hit on our behalf. Here is a man with conviction, pride and integrity. A man who is our moral and political compass. A man who stands here as a hero and a role model, not only to his beloved son, but to mine as well. Mr. Ramos, please stand up and be recognized."

The whooping and hollering from the audience rises to the ceiling as Mr. Ramos takes his bow. Mrs. Ramos gives him a peck on the cheek and Mr. Sandoval walks over to give the man a handshake and a manly embrace.

"I think I'm going to be sick," I say.

Lib comes back to share in the shock. "Now *this* is too much. A role model, huh? Boy, Mr. Sandoval can lay it on as thick as eyeshadow on a street walker."

Trini looks a bit befuddled but she joins in the applause. As does Sebastián, but with less enthusiasm. Even my father realizes the extent of the farce, but he has no choice: Mr. Ramos, overcome with emotion, looks like he's about to weep. So does Mr. Benson. Imagine, so much love at Las Cazuelas on Cinco de Mayo. It's affection on a historical-international scale.

The mariachi band comes in to save the day with a cheery number that allows people to relax their excitement. The pitchers of margaritas start flowing and there are so many baskets of chips up in the air as the busboys weave their way through the crowded floor that it looks as if it's a Mexican folk dance of some kind.

Once the conga line to the buffet starts to get long, Trini comes over to join Lib and me at the front.

"Evening, señoritas," she says. "Are those new guayabera blouses you're wearing? *Love* the color."

"Trini," I say. "I'm so sorry."

Trini's eyes widen. "Sorry? About what?"

Lib chimes in. "Hello. Was it my imagination or did your father just get crowned Man of the Year."

"Wonderful, isn't it?" Trini says. "And Mr. Sandoval's been so generous with us. He even provided one of his hot-shot lawyers from Orange County to bail my father out."

"Money is power," Lib whispers under his breath.

"Who are we today, Lib? Supreme Court Justice Sonia Sotomayor?" Trini says. "I do hope you're not making judgments against Mr. Sandoval. He's become a close friend of the family now."

I balk. "Not to be disrespectful but—"

"Then, don't be," Trini breaks in. "Look, I know what you two bitches are thinking, I could see you making Picasso faces from across the room. But this isn't about me, it's about my father and how he's finally doing some good for a change. And I believe in giving him a chance. So do me a huge favor, you petty pubic hairs: stop getting all righteous and stop spray-painting my father's trophies. Now, show me back to my table, hostess."

"You can follow the baloney crumbs all the way back to the performing stage, miss," I say.

Trini gives me the once-over and then walks away.

"Geez, Maui," Lib says. "Are you two going to undo the stitches on the prom dress all over again?"

"I don't get it, Lib," Maui says. "Why is she pretending like that?"

Lib shakes his head. "I don't know. But maybe she's right and Mr. Ramos does deserve a second chance. Maybe we're being too judgmental? If Trini can forgive him, then why can't we?"

My head hurts. This one keeps getting more and more complicated. But regardless of what I think I'll have to apologize to Trini eventually, otherwise I'll put our friendship in peril again. And this time, I don't know if we'll be able to mend it.

The partying continues without wavering for the next few hours until the guests start slowing down their intake of alcohol and refried beans. By this time, Lib has closed the curio market and been picked up by Mr. García, who popped his head in for a quick hello. Not long after, Maddy and Snake are the first to leave.

"Good night, Mauricio," Maddy says. "Please tell Mickey to come by my place later this week to pick up some pictures from the baby shower. There are some fun ones in there with the girls."

"Will do," I say. I lower my head to speak to Maddy's belly. "Good night, Robbie!"

"Later, dude," Snake says, giving me a fist bump.

It was odd that Maddy didn't feel weird about mentioning the girls since one of them was Sandra, the leader of the other side to this demonstration conflict. Maybe this forgiveness thing is not a bad way to go after all.

When it's their turn to leave, Mrs. Ramos and Trini have to hold Mr. Ramos up from both sides. Mr. Sandoval escorts them all the way to the restaurant exit.

"You take tomorrow off, buddy," Mr. Sandoval says. Mr. Ramos grunts. So then Mr. Sandoval addresses Mrs. Ramos: "He can stay home tomorrow and sleep it off. He's had a long day."

"Thank you, Mr. Sandoval," Mrs. Ramos says.

"Please," he objects. "It's Francisco."

"Good night, Francisco," she says, and they head out the door. "And good night to you too, Maui," she calls out as an afterthought.

Trini and I don't exchange pleasantries. It's too soon for that. We have to make nice first.

"Need a lift home?" Sebastián says, coming up behind me.

"You look like you've weathered this storm all right," I say. Indeed, he looks just as fresh as when he first walked in. When he smiles, there's not even a trace of Mexican food on his teeth!

"I've been to many of these functions before," he says. "I just get in the zone and don't come back until it's over. Well, what do you say? Need some company?"

"You're as fine as flan," I say. "And, yes, I could use some dessert."

When I tell my father I'm getting a lift home, he's so distracted he doesn't bother to ask with whom, which is exactly what I counted on. Las Cazuelas has cleared out plenty by then, and Yolanda has wormed her way to the table of honor, which Mr. Benson doesn't object to since it's clear by his gushing that Mr. Sandoval likes the arm candy.

"Nice night to look at the stars," Sebastián says as soon as we're in the parking lot.

Indeed, the sky is clear and I'm already anticipating the view from Chiriaco Summit. But instead of heading up the canyon, Sebastián drives south on Highway 111.

"Are you going to smuggle me into Mexico?" I joke.

Sebastián smiles. "Kind of."

About thirty minutes later, one-third of the way to the international border, we reach a clearing, one of the few stretches of land in the Caliente Valley that's not being razed for development by Sandoval Construction. Under the moonlight the salty topsoil looks as if it's glowing, and the few growths of dusty brush shimmer and sparkle like glass.

"Diamonds in the sky, diamonds in the dirt," Sebastián says.

"Sounds like you're writing a poem," I say.

"That's the real poetry, out there," he says, pointing. "Don't you think it's tragic that we cover up this natural beauty with our man-made atrocities?"

"And don't you think it's ironic that that's how your father made the money to buy you this schmancy car?"

"Easy," Sebastián warns me. "We still have the long drive back."

"Sorry."

But he's right. We get out and lean on the car, side by side, as we take in the unsullied state of nature, before the bulldozers, before the paved roads and tract housing, before the burial beneath cement and artificial turf. Sebastián puts his arm around me and nudges the top of my head. I face him and allow him to kiss me.

"This is the only thing that's real," he says.

I don't know if he means our affection for each other, or the desert's glory, or this moment, but I don't want to ruin the intimacy with a request for a clarification. Sometimes I just need to let things stand as they are.

"Hey, so despite the fact that Trini and I are having this off-again/on-again friendship, we're still going forward with the prom plot," I say.

Sebastián keeps looking out into the open, still captivated by the view. "That's good. I'm counting on it."

"What are you counting on?" I ask.

"I'm counting on making our statement," he says.

"Yeah, well, lately those things haven't been working out for people. It's what created this whole demonstration fiasco. The consequences of that day are going to be haunting us for a while. So anyway, I have a favor to ask."

Sebastián finally turns to look at me. "Ask."

"Would you be our entry for Prom King?"

He laughs. "Me? Prom King? Why can't you do it? What about Lib?"

"Let's face it. If the senior class has to vote for a dreamboat, they'd vote for you, even if it meant voting for Trini by association. It would be our only chance to actually get some votes. Who knows? We might even win!"

I hadn't voiced the strategy until that moment, and now that I have I'm suddenly excited by it.

"What do you say, Prince Charming? You game?"

After a brief hesitation, Sebastián nods his head. "Okay," he says. "But only if you give me another kiss."

And then we kiss, not in the shadows of the back seat or hiding behind a closed door, but right there in the shamelessness of broad moonlight. For the first time I feel as if this is love. Yes, it is. I'm in love. Sebastián is my first true reciprocal love. Dare I go the next step? Dare I allow him to reach into my clothes and take whatever he wants? Dare I offer it to him?

Oh, who wants answers, when it's the questions and their dance toward possibility that keep me breathless.

BFF

The next morning, I wake up naked in Sebastián's arms. Yeah, right. Just checking to see if you're paying attention. Actually, the next morning, I wake up with the smell of nacho cheese in my hair and I'm grossed out that last night I fell in love in that condition. My alarm rings at seven in the morning and I'm still tired from all the activity last night—my legs, my heart, my lips. Nonetheless, I drag myself out of bed, put on my school uniform (sneakers, jeans and a t-shirt), and rush to the bus stop with a piece of Mexican sweet bread in my hand. I get to leave crumbs all over the bus.

When I get to the Queer Planter, Lib is already sitting there with a copy of *The Red and the Black*.

"You know, this book is sexier than *East of Eden* and it was published like a hundred and twenty years before Steinbeck's," he says. "Of course, they're both about how ambitious and manipulative we human beings can be. Sounds like we don't change much."

"Where's Sebastián?" I ask, looking around.

Lib puts the book down and glares at me. "Hi. Good morning to you too. Am I less interesting without Sebastián here?"

"Sorry, girl, that was rude. Let me start over," I say, and then I slip into my chipper mode: "Hi, Lib! I see Sebastián let you borrow his book. Where is he by the way?"

"I prefer your more honest entrance," Lib says. "For your information, Trini and Sebastián went to sign up for prom court since today's the last day to do so."

"Really? Wow," I say. I'm slightly hurt that I'm not leading the expedition.

"Don't get jealous now," Lib says.

I shake my head. "Me, jealous?"

"I mean, it makes sense. Trini's going to wear the dress and if you or I were to be her date that would be like incest or something, so it's better for her to take someone outside of the Caliente Valley gene pool."

"Gotcha," I say, annoyed that he's taking credit for what I came up with last night.

When Trini and Sebastián return, Trini skipping like Jill going up the hill to fetch a pail of water, I get two disparate receptions. Sebastián is thrilled to find me here; Trini, not so thrilled.

"Good morning, Mauricio," she says.

I respond in kind: "Good morning, Trinidad."

"Uh-oh," Lib says, fanning himself. "Long names. Bad sign."

"Hey, you two," Sebastián steps in, putting one arm over my shoulder and one arm over Trini's. "No nonsense, okay. We just moved one step closer to our plan. We're signed up for the prom court! This is a time to celebrate, not deprecate."

"Nice bumper sticker," Lib says. Sebastián winks.

"Well," Trini says. "As usual I have to be the better person here and take the first step toward a truce."

My eyes narrow, but both Sebastián and Lib give me the grin-and-bear-it look, so I keep my mouth shut. Besides, I deserve it. This time.

"You're right, Trini. I was way out of line with the things I said last night, I'm sorry. So I agree to this truce, but only if you accept my apology first."

Trini pretends to look around her, stalling before giving her answer. "Fine," she says finally, leaning over to give me a hug. "But only because I'm too excited to stay angry. My gown's finished and I want you all to come over to the Glamorous Grotto this weekend for the big unveiling."

Lib rubs his hands together. "*Fabulous*, a dress debut!"

Trini turns to Sebastián. "And you take notes. I want you to color coordinate your tux with my gown and to pick out the right corsage. Nothing cheap from the grocery store, either."

Sebastián chuckles. "Yes, ma'am!"

When the bell rings, Lib packs up his book and heads to the classroom walking next to Sebastián. I hold Trini back with my hand. When the others turn around, I wave them away. They know what it's all about.

"Yes, Maui?" Trini asks. "Can't it wait until study hour?"

I shake my head. "Trini, I want to give you a proper apology. You've been so generous and forgiving of me all these years, even though I keep being a real pain on your behind. And I want to thank you for not giving up on me, for continuing to be my friend even through the rough times. You're a wonderful human being, and the best friend I will ever have."

Trini wipes a tear from her eye. "Oh, Maui, look at what you've done to me. I'm going to walk into remedial English with the face of a raccoon! You know I love you, Passion Flower. Even though sometimes your petals stink. But no matter what, we'll always be BFF."

"BFF," I say.

"All right, let's bolt before we're late!" she says, and we part ways to reach our respective home rooms before the tardy bell rings.

I fade in and out for the rest of the day, thinking about the upcoming prom and graduation and the day after. Everything's going to slip through our fingers in less than a month. And then what? I mean, I know there's college in the fall, but what about that period between high school graduation and college? It seems kind of lame to simply go full time at Las Cazuelas. Sebastián will take off to New York City and I'll probably never see him again. And what of Trini? Being BFF is going to be tough once I too move out of Caliente. Oh, I wish high school math were more interesting so that I wouldn't have to dwell on these things!

It's in the middle of my existential dilemmas that I'm forced to snap to attention when a special announcement is made over the intercom in which Principal Beasley names the class valedictorian. It's no surprise: Liberace García.

Ms. Lemmons gets the applause going and Lib just sits there grinning like a Halloween pumpkin. Even the jocks who have never even talked to us before reach over to give him a few pats on the back.

"Congrats, Lib," Sebastián says.

I want to walk up and hug him, but instead I sit there and get all misty-eyed: our baby mariposa is all grown up.

"I hope you will remember us when you're out there doing great things, Liberace," Ms. Lemmons says.

As soon as we're dismissed for the day, I reach over to tousle Lib's hair.

"Hey," he says. "What's that for?"

"Just," I say. "I'm so frickin' proud of you. Wait until your parents find out. Wait until I tell my father and Mr. Benson. I bet they throw you a party!"

"Relax," Lib says. "It's only the highest honor to be given to a high school student, that's all."

"Silly goose!" I say, and tousle his hair again.

"Well, if your bosses don't throw you a party, we will," Sebastián says. "I think we should definitely combine Trini's unveiling with Lib's academic distinction, don't you think?"

"Why not?" I say, though with a little apprehension. "I'll get Mickey to bake a cake for the occasion."

"What kind?" Sebastián asks.

Lib and I chuckle. "Fruitcake!"

The news of Lib getting named class valedictorian is well received at Las Cazuelas, and both Mr. Gutiérrez and Mr. Benson come out to shake his hand. A few customers who happen to be within earshot also come over to congratulate Lib. Funny looking or not, the kid's smart. Yolanda is so impressed that when she comes back from her cigarette break she tells Lib that her now-ex-boyfriend offered his congratulations. All the while Lib looks like he's floating on clouds, and his silly grin remains fixed on his face until closing time, and when Mr. García comes in to pick him up, he bursts into proud tears when Lib tells him.

I burst into tears as well. Geez, what's the matter with me, I'm so emotional lately. Mr. Benson comes out to shake Mr. García's hand for raising such a fine, intelligent boy.

And that's when it stings. I'm ashamed to admit it, but I'm suddenly feeling a little left out of the limelight. Let me put it in perspective: Trini's probably going to make history by becoming Caliente Valley High School's first-ever cross-gender Prom Queen, and Lib is once again thrust into the center of admiration by becoming our resident Goth valedictorian. Where does that leave me? Oh, crap. I'm average.

The word weighs on me all the way home in the back seat of Mr. García's car as he yammers on and on about how this is a watershed moment in the family line and how Lib will be receiving a call from Harvard or Yale begging him to enroll in their prestigious university. It's so over-the-top I want to plug my ears.

And just as quickly I plummet into the guilt: I should celebrate, not deprecate!

I'm dropped off at home and I crawl like the insect I am into the house, only to be greeted by my sister in tears on the couch. It's going to be another long night.

"What's the matter, Mickey?"

"Nothing," she says.

"Okay," I say, thinking she's giving me an easy way out, but before I even make it across the room she stops me.

"Maui," she says. "Sandra and I had another ugly fight."

I spin on my heels and then take my place next to her on the couch. I hold her hand.

"Tell me all about it, sis," I say, prepared to listen to another epic tale of friendship and betrayal.

Mrs. Sandoval

All is calm and all is bright for the rest of the week until word leaks out on Friday afternoon at Las Cazuelas that tonight Mr. Sandoval will have a special guest for dinner: Mrs. Sandoval. Yolanda's hackles rise.

"I bet she's a real witch," she says, puckering her lips slightly. "Only a witch would leech on a prize like Francisco and then toss him out like a banana peel after she's done with him."

I've been standing next to Yolanda for months now, that I think I've earned the right to banter. "So," I say. "You're mad that you didn't glob onto him first?"

Yolanda turns to me and wobbles her head a little. "Exactly."

Mr. Benson puts on his favorite tie, even though there isn't really any special function scheduled, and Mr. Gutiérrez orders that Mr. Sandoval's table be accentuated with real flowers. The server walks away looking troubled. When he passes us he remarks, "And where am I supposed to get these flowers?"

Somehow, a small but pleasant bouquet materializes and is stuffed inside a decorative vase from the Mexican curio market. Lib reluctantly relinquishes the vase.

"I'm not going to be able to sell that used!" he calls out when the server takes the vase.

For the rest of us it's business as usual until Mr. Sandoval and Sebastián walk in. When he realizes his wife is fashionably late, Mr. Sandoval gets on his iPhone to track her down.

Sebastián rolls his eyes and leans in close to me. "It's a game they like to play: she doesn't respond until he starts imagining the worst, and then she shows up pretending she wasn't doing this to edge him closer to a heart attack. He hates to be kept waiting."

"You wait for your mother here, Sebastián," Mr. Sandoval says. "Let me go chat with the boys for a few minutes."

"I'll take you there, Mr. Sandoval," Yolanda says, and she takes the lead as they walk away.

Sebastián and I make eye contact. We know what chatting with the boys means: throwing back a few shots. And since I'm on that wavelength, I detect the lingering odor of alcohol. At first I think it's Mr. Sandoval, but he would've taken the scent with him. That narrows down the list of suspects.

"You've been drinking?" I whisper to Sebastián.

He holds up his thumb and forefinger to indicate "only a little bit."

"Don't you think your parents will notice?"

Sebastian balks. "Right," he says. "Only if they're able to detect my booze breath through theirs."

"Still," I say. "Lay off the stuff, will you? It could become a bad habit."

Sebastián's eyes soften and I'm suddenly plunged back into our private moments of lip-locking and caressing. I would've stayed suspended in the memory for much longer, but then we're interrupted by the grand lady making her entrance.

How to describe Mrs. Sandoval? Well, she looks like she spends half of her day in the beauty parlor, fluffing that head full of hair, and the other half on a stationary bike, working out her killer calves. Trini would be floored by the fierce outfit: a tight-fitting white skirt, a matching blouse with a sharp oversized collar, and a thick belt that cinches her tiny waist like a corset. Yolanda might say she looks like a wasp, but I say she looks like she's been beamed out of some fancy cocktail party in L.A. and, to her dismay, been teleported to our humble Mexican restaurant.

"Welcome to Las Cazuelas," I say. Behind me the fajitas sizzle and the blender crushes ice into a daiquiri.

Mrs. Sandoval looks around and does a double take when she spots Lib behind the counter in the curio market. He smiles and waves. Her eyes move to the top of her head—this is quite a cross for her to bear.

"Mom," Sebastián says, shaking Mrs. Sandoval out of her initial shock.

Her entire disposition changes when she sees her son. She tips her head to one side and kisses him on the cheek. "Sebastián, querido," she says. And just as quickly she becomes alarmed. "Who's been cutting your hair? And I *know* there are nicer shoes in the closet than those."

Sebastián grins, slightly embarrassed. "Mom, please. I want you to meet my friend, Maui."

She looks at me and smiles.

"We're close," he adds, and then her smile fades.

"Is that right?" she says. "Maui. Are you Hawaiian?"

I laugh. "No, it's short for Mauricio. It's Mexican."

"Well, then, Mauricio is a perfectly dignified name. Don't you have any pride in your Mexican heritage? I don't allow Sebastián to be anything but Sebastián—it shows strength of character and respect for his Argentinian, Italian *and* Mexican ancestry."

"Mom, please," Sebastián pleads. "And that's Lib over there."

Reluctantly, Mrs. Sandoval turns toward Lib again, and Lib calls out from a distance, "Hi! That's short for Liberace."

She doesn't seem amused, so she turns back to Sebastián. "Where's your father? I want to get this over with. I've a massage, a hot tub and a martini waiting for me in Palm Springs."

"Mom, there are some perfectly nice hotels here in Caliente," Sebastián says.

"I hear there's free cable at the Palm Tree Hotel off Van Buren Boulevard," I offer.

"How nice," she says. "Sebastián. Your father?"

"I can take you there, Mrs. Sandoval," I say. "Follow me."

When we arrive to Mr. Sandoval's table, it's like he totally forgot his ex-wife was coming. He sits all relaxed with Mr. Benson, Mr. Gutiérrez and Yolanda. The men all get up to receive her.

"Mrs. Sandoval," Mr. Benson says. "I'm Howard Benson, the owner of this establishment. And this is Gutiérrez, the manager. Yolanda is our hostess."

"Amelia," she says and holds out her hand for Mr. Benson. She nods to my father and to Yolanda, who looks mortified that Mrs. Sandoval looks like a million bucks.

"If you will all excuse us, gentlemen, Yolanda," Mr. Sandoval says and the party breaks up immediately.

"If there's anything you need, Amelia," Mr. Benson says before he walks away. "It's on the house."

"Thank you," Mrs. Sandoval says, a weak smile on her face.

Sebastián takes his seat and I place menus in front of all of them. "Your server will be right with you," I say. I'm not expecting a response at this point since Mr. and Mrs. Sandoval have locked gazes and are doing the fatal version of the stare-down.

"All righty, then," I say, and sneak off.

When I get back to the hostess station, Yolanda is pulling back her hair.

"How humiliating," she says. "And me with split-ends."

I'm not sure what to think about the fiery Amelia Sandoval. I'm not taking it personally since it's clear that everything is wrong with the Caliente Valley, except for her son, who's here against his will.

"I bet she's not even going to order anything," Yolanda says, running her hand over her small belly. "Women like that eat like once a week and it sounds like the only thing on her plate tonight is going to be poor Mr. Sandoval. I thought she was going to tear his throat out."

The server doesn't even have time to bring out the basket of chips when suddenly Mrs. Sandoval storms out of her seat and rushes back out to the front desk, where Sebastián finally manages to stop her.

"Mom, please," he says. "Don't do this."

Yolanda and I pretend we're busy doing other things besides eavesdropping, which is hard to do when people stand two feet away to argue.

"This was such a bad idea," she says. "I only came down here to see you since you didn't come up to West Hollywood for your uncle's book release party. He was so disappointed."

"It was a school night!" Sebastián explains.

"It was a literary event. I'm sure you could have finagled some extra credit for it or something. Lord knows you take after your father in that department. Only he could figure out a way to squeeze out the last drops of life from these unfortunate little towns."

"Mom, he's doing a lot of good here."

Mrs. Sandoval isn't hearing any of it. She opens her purse and starts digging for her car keys. "You know you have an open invitation to come back with me to New York. Just say the word. The thought of you spending one more day in this depressing place upsets my stomach."

"I only have a few weeks before graduation, Mom," he says. "Besides, I'm running for Prom King."

Mrs. Sandoval looks surprised. "Prom King?"

"Yes, we're making a huge pro-gay statement at the high school. I'm running for Prom King and my friend Trini's running for Prom Queen."

"Trini. Short for Catrina?"

I resist the urge to snicker.

"It's another guy, Mom. It's a gay thing."

"You and your gay things," Mrs. Sandoval says with derision. "Life was much simpler when you were dating girls. And these so-called pro-gay statements are what cost your father and me a fortune in legal fees at the last high school you attended, remember?" Immediately, the look of regret falls over her face. "Oh, Sebastián, I'm so sorry. I didn't mean that."

"That's all right," he says.

"No, I'm serious, that was horrible." She tries to caress his cheek but Sebastián pulls back.

"Have a safe drive back to Palm Springs, Mom," he says. "I'll see you in the summer."

Sebastián turns around and walks back to the dining table. Mrs. Sandoval, mortified, doesn't even bother saying anything and simply exits the restaurant.

"What a bitch," Yolanda says.

I'm inclined to agree. But who am I to judge my friend's parents? I think about Mr. Dutton, Mr. Ramos, and even about Mr. Gutiérrez—parenting must be complicated enough as it is. Now how about parenting a gay kid?

Mr. Sandoval's table isn't as rowdy as other Friday nights, and when they finally get up to leave, Sebastián looks tired and deflated. Lib has closed the market and sits in the waiting area with his eyes closed.

"Hey," I say to Sebastián and they head out. "See you at Trini's unveiling tomorrow?" Sebastián nods his head without enthusiasm.

I wave goodbye, and then I take a seat next to Lib.

"So, Mr. Class Valedictorian," I say. "Did you ask for the day off so that we can celebrate tomorrow?"

Lib doesn't bother opening his eyes. "Yep. One of the cashiers in the back is filling in. Was it my imagination or did some crazy lady from Melrose Place just come in to spit all over our restaurant floor?"

I exhale deeply. Who knew that all this time high school was really just another name for a support group for adolescents with troubled parents?

Suddenly I get a pang in my throat. Tomorrow is Mexican Mothers Day. And I'm kind of glad I won't be at work to see Mr. Benson exploit that holiday to draw in the Mexican crowd. I suppose it wouldn't really matter what kind of mother Mrs. Sandoval is. She's still a mother, still alive, still around for Sebastián whenever he needs her. Only those of us without mothers know the emptiness of calling out into the dark and getting no reply.

Changing Plans

On Saturday morning, I wake up in my guayabera and my tighty whities. Gross to fall asleep in my work shirt but the nights are kind of cool for this time of year in the desert. Every time the TV is on some doomsayer's talking about global warming and how humanity has so completely screwed up the ecosystem that we're probably ushering in our own extinction. Great, the end of the world. Just one more thing to worry about before I turn eighteen.

The Mariposa Club has opted to boycott Senior Trip since it's not much of a trip anyway, but an all-day excursion at the water park. Lame! So that means that on Monday we get to spend the entire day by ourselves and with any other outsider who either didn't want to go or wasn't allowed to go because they have some high school criminal record of suspensions and unexcused absences. I can hardly wait.

A knock on the door startles me into covering myself up, from the waist down at least.

"Who is it?" I say.

"It's me," Mickey says. "Can I come in?"

"Absolutely not, I'm not decent. What is it? Is the cake ready?"

"Almost. Listen, get dressed and come out here. I've got something to discuss with you. About college."

"Give me a minute," I say.

I get up, change into something more casual and come out of my room. The smell of eggs and bacon assaults my senses. Shit, she's got something else cooking besides the celebration cake for Trini and Lib.

"I made you an omelet," Mickey says, sweetly.

My body stiffens. I hate it when she does this.

"Let's just get it over with, sis," I say, sitting down at the table in front of my serving. "What gives this time?"

"Well, all right, but eat the damn omelet at least, it took me like two tries to get it right."

"Thanks," I say. I pick up the glass of orange juice and take a sip.

"I want us to live together when we move to Riverside," she says.

I choke on my juice. "Wait a minute…we've already gone over this and we agreed that we *wouldn't* be roommates, remember? You're moving in with Sandra and Janet, and I get to go to the dorms."

Mickey sighs. "I know, but things have changed since those plans were made. Janet and I are going apartment-hunting in the summer and we were checking out some of these spaces online and the ones we want are these townhouses, but they're made for at least three residents."

"What happened to Sandra? Don't tell me you guys couldn't patch things up after all that drama?"

"It's more complicated than what went on between us," Mickey says. "For some reason, this whole demonstration thing got Sandra all riled up about how the Caliente Valley needs her, especially since it seems like Sandoval Construction is going to be sticking around for a while. So, she decided that she will too."

"That's noble, but kind of crazy, isn't it? She's going to give up her future for some political agenda?" I dig into my omelet, which tastes better than it looks. Wouldn't be a bad idea to live with someone who *kind of* knows how to cook.

"I don't think she's giving anything up, only delaying it. She's deferring her enrollment at the university until next year."

I bite into a piece of crunchy bacon. Yummy. "Well, let me think about it. I don't have to decide right now, do I?"

"No, I'm just throwing it out there now instead of pressuring you later."

"Thanks," I say. "I have to talk to Lib. Any chance we could *both* move in with you and Janet? We could share a room."

Mickey ponders it for a moment. "That wouldn't be such a bad idea, either. Let me discuss it with Janet and get back to you on that one. See? That wasn't too bad. It's all talk for now, that's all."

"That's all," I say, and return to my breakfast.

At this point, Papi comes out of his room looking exhausted at the exact moment Mickey pulls the small cake out of the oven. He looks puzzled by the spread on the table, but pounces on it before he heads off to work. "Any toast?" he asks.

After Mickey and I spread the chocolate frosting on the cake, I pretty much veg on a full stomach in the quiet of the living room for the next couple of hours before Sebastián comes by at noon. Lib is supposed to meet me here at about the same time, so I'm surprised when there's a knock at the door at eleven. Mickey's in her room, Papi's already left for Las Cazuelas, so I have to haul my butt off the couch to answer it.

"Hi, Maui," Lib says.

I look at my watch. "Is it Daylight Savings Time already?"

"No, I'm early," he says. "I wanted to discuss something with you." He bites his lip and the ring sticks out a little.

What is in the air this morning? I signal with my head for him to enter and then I stretch my arm out to direct him to the couch.

"You want anything to drink?" I ask.

"You've got like a milkshake or a smoothie?"

"How about I give you an orange and you bite into it while jumping on one foot?"

"I'm okay, thanks, Ms. Congeniality," he says.

"I'm kidding," I say. I go to the fridge and bring out a pair of sodas for us.

He takes his and holds it on his lap. His face remains expressionless.

"You're making me nervous, Lib."

"I don't know where to start," he says.

"Just spit it out and then we'll peel it like an artichoke."

"I've decided *not* to go to UC Riverside," he says.

All I have to say is that I thank my lucky stars I have the healthy heart of a seventeen year old, otherwise it would've imploded by now. I mean, I know the school drop-out rate for Latinos is staggeringly high, but who ever heard of dropping out of college before you even drop in?

"Let me guess?" I say. "You're going to enroll in the local community college." I scratch the back of my ear.

"Actually, I'm still going to college, just not any college here in California," he says. "I'm going to Dartmouth. An Ivy League school."

"Dartmouth? Where the hell is *that*?"

"New Hampshire."

"New Hampshire?" I say. "Where the hell is *that*?"

"Maui, the point is that I want you to be okay with this decision. I know that we swore to each other that we were going to stick together and attend the same school, but I got offered this amazing scholarship and it was hard to turn down an all-expense-paid education to such a prestigious institution, especially because my parents can't afford to give me a single dime."

I grin. "I'm fine with this, Lib, you know it was really you who had been insisting on us following the same path, and it was always me saying that you were meant for better things."

Lib leans over to hug me. "Thank you, Maui, this means so much to me."

I can't help but feel like he punched my heart right out of my chest cavity though. This morning I was suggesting to Mickey that Lib could be my roommate and now I find out we're going to be living on opposite sides of the country. Wow.

"There's one more thing," he says.

"Be gentle," I say.

"I have to use your phone to call your father at Las Cazuelas. I'm going to need a few more days off since Dartmouth College is flying my parents and me to the east coast to check out my new digs. I'm so excited about it!"

I point to the phone in the kitchen. To avoid having to hear this whole spiel again I turn on the TV. Global warming. Maybe the world will end this summer and I won't have to worry about what's expected of me in September when I move in with Mickey and Janet—three single college students seeking a career and a love life.

I don't even bother bringing up the whole roommate situation in Riverside since it's a dead horse. And when Mickey comes out of her room she's in such a hurry to leave she doesn't bring it up either, to my relief. So Lib and I sit and watch some nonsense on the TV until Sebastián comes to pick us up.

"Can we ride with the top down?" Lib asks and Sebastián complies, which makes it hard to have a conversation on our way to

Trini's but that's all right. Neither Sebastián or I have much to say. We've both been rattled by our loved ones enough in the last twenty-four hours.

When we get to the Glamorous Grotto, I carry the cake and Lib knocks. Trini, in full makeup and face glitter, and wrapped in a silk robe, peeks out.

"Welcome to the premiere of the paradise gown by Chez Treenée," she says. "That's double *e*, double *e*."

"Silly faggot," Lib says. "French is for flamers."

"This should be fun," Sebastián quips.

Trini, or Treenée rather, opens the door slowly and we walk in. The lights are dimmed, and she's decorated the bare walls with Aunt Carmen's fringed shawls. She moved the furniture around to affect a runway, although this catwalk is going to be nothing longer than a six-foot stretch across the shed.

"Sit down, distinguished guests," she says to Sebastián and me. "And goblins," she says when she looks at Lib. Lib sticks out his tongue.

"I see you brought the pâté," Trini says.

"Sure," I say as I hand her the chocolate cake. It was too small to write an inscription on it, so I had Mickey draw a white butterfly.

"How quaint," she says. "Mariposa cake, my favorite. We'll scarf it down later, but only if you have room after feasting your eyes on this!"

In one swoop, Trini runs to the light switch, turns it off and leaves us in the dark for a few seconds. When the lights go back on—she's posing in the middle of the room in her prom gown. She looks over at Lib. "Don't just sit there, press the play button!"

Lib reaches over to the boom box and as soon as Lady Gaga starts singing, Trini starts sashaying.

"Should we clap or something?" Sebastián asks me.

"It will make her day," I say and get the rhythm going. The others join in right away.

The first official design in the new line by Chez Treenée is a sleek, slimming number in moonlight blue with a pattern of shiny silver sequins cascading down from the shoulders to the front of the dress. The design fools the eye into imagining that there's an actual pair of baby boobs in there and not a stuffed bra. The sequins help shape a pair of feminine thighs and then they drop down and scatter all over the hem to weigh it down. The shoes peeping out from under the gown glitter in harmony with her eye makeup. It's brilliantly executed drag wear.

"Okay, okay," Trini says. "Turn that off before my glitter starts flaking off my face. I could only afford one tiny bottle on my Wal-Mart budget."

"Incredible, Trini," I say. "You got all your materials at Wal-Mart?"

"I did," she says. "I should really skip beauty school and get into the clothing design business. Chez Treenée: *Magic Eye for Magic Nights!*"

Lib stands up to inspect it closer. "It is kind of fierce. Is it one size fits all?"

Trini rolls her eyes. "Although it's part stretch material, even Lycra has a breaking point, dear. I'd need to special order for you full-figured types."

"I meant for someone like Maui," Lib says. "You know, for people from planet Earth."

"Oh, I wouldn't wear it," I say.

"Well, thank you, hater bitches," Trini says. "I worked my ass off on this gown, I mean, look at my fingertips: I've got permanent calluses from pushing the needle night after night."

I stand up and hold Trini's hand. "That's not what I meant, Trini. I meant that I'm not the type to wear a dress. But you look fabulous in it, doesn't she, Sebastián?"

Sebastián comes to save the day. "Yes! I mean, I couldn't have asked for a prettier prom date."

Trini blushes. "Oh, thank you. Take note, ladies: that's a true gentleman for you!"

While Trini changes back into an outfit she can sit comfortably in, we pull the furniture back into place and set up our treats. The flutes are out, filled with apple cider, and the delectable mariposa cake graces the center.

Everyone takes a flute.

"We hereby hold a special meeting of the Mariposa Club," I say. "To honor our two members for their fabulous accomplishments. To Mariposa Trini, cheers to your amazing gown. She will *be* our fiercest Prom Princess. And to Mariposa Lib, cheers to your amazing fortune. He's off to Dartmouth College in the fall."

"Dartmouth?" Sebastián says. "Impressive."

"Never heard of it," Trini says. "But cheers to you, anyway."

We clink glasses, drink, and have some cake.

"How about you, Sebastián?" Lib says. "What are your plans for the fall?"

Sebastián wipes the corner of his mouth with a finger. "I'm moving to New York City, of course. But I've decided to take a year off and work, maybe do an internship in publishing. My uncle's a writer and he's got connections in the industry. After that, I'll see. I'm not in any rush."

"Good for you," Trini says. "And who knows, we might end up bumping into each other in the streets of Manhattan. They film *Project Runway* there, you know."

"Well, let's not get ahead of ourselves, Trini," I say. "I think you need a little more time with the needle and thread before you're ready for prime-time."

"Oh, you never know," Sebastián says. "Genius gets discovered in the most unusual of places."

"Hear that, Maui?" Trini says, cupping her palm around her ear. "*Genius.*"

"While I agree, Sebastián, that Trini has talent, I don't think we'd be doing her any favors if we just told her she's ready to rumble when she can still grow and evolve."

"Evolve?" Sebastián says. "What is she, a lower species?"

"Was I just insulted?" Trini asks.

Sebastián shakes his head. "I wish you'd have a little more faith in your friends. Especially those who need your support."

"Yeah, Maui," Trini says. "Celebrate, don't deprecate."

"And I wish you'd stop condescending to *my* friends," I fire back.

"Oh. My. Goddess," Lib says. "I know what this little tennis tango is all about: Maui hasn't taken a ride on Sebastián's disco stick!"

"Lib!" I protest. "That's crass."

"And very true, isn't it? You win the bet, Trini."

"You placed a bet over my sex life?" I say, horrified.

Trini swats me gently on the arm. "Oh, relax, Passion Flower. We just made a friendly wager over whether or not you had opened your kimono to Sebastián. I didn't think you had. Nothing wrong with that. Chastity's hard to come by nowadays. Although *how* you could resist is beyond me. Sebastián can melt wax just by looking at it. Woof!"

Sebastián is amused by the whole thing, but I'm not.

"Well, it's none of your business, girls," I say. "I know we share plenty, but this is one thing that's out of reach. Is that clear?"

"So clear it's pure," Trini says. And Lib chuckles.

"Let's eat more cake, you all," I say. "Ain't nothing going to eat us."

We whoop and holler some more. Though plenty of cuts have been made in the heat of the moment, we treat the wounds just as quickly. It's the ephemeral nature of our group—it will all be over when we disperse. So even those swipes that would sting for days can't be taken too seriously. There's not much time left.

Sebastián, I must add, has been a good sport. And I have the urge to surrender to him before the end of the school year. I shudder with excitement. I think I'm ready to take that step after all.

At the close of our celebration, we hug and peck, and leave the Glamorous Grotto in good spirits. Lib takes the remainder of the cake home and we drop him off because he needs to pack for his trip to Hanover, New Hampshire, tomorrow morning.

"So where do we go now?" Sebastián asks me. "It's early."

"How about back to your place," I suggest.

"My place?"

"Sure," I say. "Why not? You've been to my house but I've never been to yours. I'd like to see how the other half lives."

Sebastián seems uncertain, but then agrees to it. "Let me just text my father, first. He doesn't like surprises."

When he gets a quick response back, Sebastián smiles.

"Looks like Pops has got a date tonight," he says. "We've got the place *all* to ourselves."

"Don't get any ideas now," I warn him. "I've got enough of them for the both of us."

And with that, we take off to the only gated community in Caliente. I've never been inside of it. It'll be a night full of firsts.

Desert Oasis

First of all, what other kind of an oasis is there? Duh! And secondly, what's this claim to fame as the paradise in the middle of nowhere? I mean, yeah, we've got our barrios, our low-income housing, our working-class neighborhoods, where old couches graduate from indoor seating to outdoor seating, but please, I would hardly call this place a haven from the community's eyesores.

When we drive up to the gate and Sebastián lowers the window to punch in some code on a keypad that will make the gate swing open, I'm already unimpressed by all the hoopla just to get in. We enter the driveway and circle around a series of units. Okay, I'm kind of surprised I don't see a single cooking grill or hear a single barking dog, and I'm wondering if anyone's even home because it's as quiet as a cemetery out here. There's a communal pool that tries hard to affect the whole oasis theme. And I must admit it's kind of lovely because the lights are underwater. But other than that I don't see that many differences from the tract housing at the edge of town.

Sebastián parks in front of a garage, and we get out of the car. He points with his car keys and sets the alarm, and then he enters yet another code to unlock the front door. Geez, I suppose no one ever rushes in or out of this house like we do where I live.

Once the front door opens, it's another story. How to describe this place? I'm not the kind of person who thumbs through home decorating magazines, but I have glanced at one on occasion, like at the waiting room at the dentist's. Everything in the Sandoval home looks dusted, untouched and posed. The couch, a big white dune, doesn't seem to have a single memory of a butt print, and the dining table is one long polished piece of wood that has yet to function as a dining table.

"Nice digs," I say.

"I don't hang out here at all," Sebastián says. "Neither does my father. He hides out in the den and I hide out in my room. Come on."

I follow him past the fancy kitchen, where every appliance stands to attention, spit shined and square shouldered, past a bathroom with a tub the size of my father's Cadillac, and up the stairs with suspended rungs. On the second floor, most of the doors are closed, except for his bedroom, which is what my bedroom would look like if we were to tear down a few walls.

The room is tidy, but it's obvious that Sebastián doesn't pick up his own dirty socks or collect the pizza crusts from his desk. The hired housekeeper/gourmet cook, he admits, comes in every other day. On one side of the room he stacks all of his technology: Mac, flat-screen TV, CD/DVD system, Wii, iPod, iPad, etc. Not a single poster in sight. He's actually got *real* canvas paintings on display.

"Please don't tell me you painted that," I say, pointing at a rather hard-to-define piece next to his bed. The strokes are dark and violent—it's a chaos of color and texture buzzing inside the frame.

"Nope," Sebastián says, throwing his car keys on a glass. "I didn't want that in here but my father didn't know where else to put it. Not enough space for all of his art. That piece is by a Chicano artist. Gronk."

"Gronk?" I say. "Doesn't sound very Chicano to me."

"Pops has got all the essentials—Malaquías Montoya, Rupert García."

The glass window is actually a sliding door that opens to a balcony. I move the blinds to the side with my hand.

"We can take a look," he says.

I slide the door open and step out. The balcony overlooks a construction site.

"Is that what all the fuss was about?" I ask.

Sebastián comes up behind me and wraps his arms around my torso. "I believe so. Sandoval Construction is building more housing, a strip mall. And I think a spa."

I snicker. "That's a failing enterprise. Nobody around here can afford a spa."

"The truth is it's not for the people around here. The cheaper housing and lower cost of living is going to attract people who need to downgrade a notch, which is still a few notches above the incomes of Caliente Valley residents."

My body chills. "That's horrible. This is going to make us look even poorer."

"Hey," Sebastián says. "That's America."

"That sucks," I say.

I suddenly understand Sandra's impulse to stay behind and fight. But that still won't stop me from leaving. Not all of us can make good soldiers. And I'm still having a hard time seeing Mr. Sandoval as the evil capitalist he's being made out to be, although his own perspective is questionable given how he couldn't see the other side of Mr. Ramos. I guess that's the problem with all of us—our refusal to recognize our complexities. It's easier to attack just a small part of who people really are.

Sebastián brings his head down to my neck and I feel as if I'm about to burst right out of my skin.

"You want to go inside?" he asks.

"Yes," I say. My knees began to shake. "No."

"Well, which is it?"

"First I have to ask you about something we haven't talked about. It's important for us to be honest and truthful with each other, otherwise I won't feel right about it."

Sebastián gives me an inquisitive look. "Okay, ask me anything."

"Remember when you told me about what happened in your previous high school? About the fire at the gym?"

"I do."

"I just want to know: were you *really* intending to hurt somebody or was it just an accident?"

Sebastián takes a deep breath. "Ah, yes, the infamous fire at the gym. I'd be lying if I said I wasn't intending to cause some damage, but it was only supposed to be structural. A few friends of mine and I had a run-in with some of the basketball jocks and we wanted to teach them a lesson, by disrupting their most important game. The week before they had vandalized our memorial shrine to all the young people who had committed suicide because they had been bullied in school for being gay, so it was a particularly violent affront to our cause. We just wanted to short-circuit the wiring, but something went wrong and it started a fire. People got hurt and we regretted that. I took the fall because unlike my accomplices I had father who had clout and could get me out of it. And the rest is history. So no, I'm not a psycho, Maui. But neither am I a saint."

"You seemed so cold and tough-guy about it when you first mentioned it to me."

"I was putting on airs back then, trying to impress you. But this is the truth."

I kiss him on the lips. "I believe you."

We walk all the way to the edge of the bed and he peels my shirt off. But there's something about the large room and the glass door that makes me ask him to kill the lights. When his body presses next to mine again, it's now skin against skin.

What happens next is, well, none of your business. Just like I told the girls, I know that we share plenty but this is one thing that's out of reach. Losing your virginity is not talked about, it's experienced, and it's a private chapter in everyone's book. Unfortunately, not a single page gets to be written tonight. Let's just say that as things get a little hot and heavy, the house alarm goes off.

Startled, Sebastián pulls away.

"Is someone breaking in?" I say.

We quickly rise from the bed and start searching for our clothes in the dark.

"I can't see anything," I say.

"I'm not turning the light on," Sebastián says. "It could be an intruder."

Somehow we get dressed and we creep over to the door to crack it open.

"Maybe you should call the police," I say.

"We have our own security here. They should be here any minute."

And that's when we hear the commotion downstairs. It's Mr. Sandoval speaking loudly with the security guard.

"What's he doing home?" Sebastián says. He opens the door and I follow him down to the living room.

By this time the alarm has been deactivated and the security guards turn to leave, but the fun is just about to start, because standing next to a tipsy Mr. Sandoval is a tipsy Yolanda. And that's when I notice that not only are Sebastián and I wearing each other's shirts, we're wearing them inside out. *Awkward!*

"Dad," Sebastián says. "Did you forget the code again?"

"Oh, hello," he says. "What are you doing here?"

"What are *you* doing here? You said you were on a date," says Sebastián.

This sobers up Mr. Sandoval a bit because his face flushes. "I am," he says. "Yolanda, this is my son."

Yolanda looks embarrassed, which is a look I know I'm currently displaying also.

"We've met," she says.

"Oh, that's right, that's right," Mr. Sandoval says. "So that means you also know Maui."

I grin. "She sure does," I say.

"Well." Mr. Sandoval says after another uncomfortable silence. "Since our parties have collided how about we all have a little sit down and have a cup of coffee or something?"

Sebastián shakes his head. "Our guests can relax on the couch. We'll prepare some coffee and tea. Dad?"

Mr. Sandoval excuses himself and follows Sebastián to the kitchen.

Yolanda and I stare at each other until we burst into giggles, covering our mouths to muffle them.

"Fancy seeing you on your day off," she says, breaking the ice.

"This is sad," I say. "It just goes to show you how small the dating pool is in our beloved Caliente."

"Too funny," she says. "At least it's all out in the open. There's nothing worse than running around pretending and denying. Besides, if anything we should be high-fiving, Maui. These are the catches of the year."

I smile and high-five, knowing well that unlike Mr. Sandoval, Sebastián did not move here to stay and will be taking off right after graduation, which happens in just a few weeks.

When the Sandovals return they carry in a tray with coffee for the grown-ups, tea for the teenagers, and a small but appetizing selection of fruit, cheese and butter cookies. We sit around the coffee table like it was just another evening at Las Cazuelas, except that we're in the Desert Oasis and it doesn't smell like melted cheddar and beans. And then Mr. Sandoval has the bright idea of playing cards, so we clear the coffee table and play a few rounds of poker to humor him. It's clear that he's a lonely man and that nothing pleases him more than having company. When I catch him looking at his son, I detect a deep sadness in his eyes and it hits me right in the center of the heart. *Of course* Mr. Sandoval is sad. In just a few weeks he will lose his son. And I think about Mr. García and about my father. Well, I'll be a drag queen's auntie. Rich man, poor man, they've got the same kinds of hurt to contend with.

As the evening winds down and I yawn, Sebastián suggests that it's time to take me home, which I'm grateful for. I shake Mr. Sandoval's hand and kiss Yolanda on the cheek, letting her know that I'll see her tomorrow at work, and that we don't have to speak about it to anyone. She winks.

On the way back to my neighborhood, Sebastián takes my hand in the car.

"Sorry we got interrupted," he says.

"That's all right," I say. "It's probably better that way."

"What do you mean? You didn't want to?"

I choose my words carefully. "I did, I swear to you. But I'm kind of relieved we didn't. It's one of the few things I'll be able to hold on to for a while longer. Everything else is slipping out of my hands."

“You can be so philosophical, Maui,” Sebastián says. “That’s why I like you so much.”

When we get to the driveway, Sebastián parks and turns off the ignition, an echo of my drives with Isaac, who I haven’t thought about in so long.

“Good night. Sebastián,” I say. I lean over to kiss him. He presses his lips to mine.

“Good night,” he says.

I get out of the car, and then he backs out and drives away. In that kiss I think it was made clear that there would be no more nights like the one we almost had. And for the first time I feel that I’ve got something to be proud of, something I have complete control over, something that’s mine and mine alone.

Senior Tripping

Sunday brunch comes and goes. I ask Yolanda no questions and she tells me no lies about what transpired between her and Mr. Sandoval after Sebastián and I left the house. But let's just say that she seemed quite happy, with a glow about her that didn't die down with the workday.

On Monday, I'm the only senior on the school bus, and the Queer Planter is short one member since Lib's still out visiting his future college on the east coast. This doesn't seem to faze Trini, who goes on and on about this new design she's cooking up. Sebastián and I listen patiently and I suspect that, when Lib returns, we'll have to sit through another one of these sessions as Lib tells us all about his visit.

Because the Senior Quad is empty, the underclassmen invade it, getting a taste of what's going to be theirs eventually. I can't help but feel a strange sense of territoriality and I want to go over and shoo them away like pigeons.

"Look at these vultures," Trini says. "We're not even cold in the grave and they're already moving in."

"The way of the world, I suppose," Sebastián chimes in.

Trini and I look at each other and exchange the same telepathic thought: *Isn't he precious?*

Three girls in heavy makeup and tight t-shirts walk by. One of them, who looks slightly familiar, turns around and gives us the plucked eagle eye. Trini gets all defensive.

"Keep it in the socket, girlfriend," she calls out. This makes the girl scowl.

"Trini," I say. "Don't start anything. They're like, gangster girlfriends or something."

"I don't give a rat's ass," she says. "She was spending so much time on my face I was ready to charge her rent!"

Sebastián laughs and I frown. "Don't encourage her," I say.

Because the classes are mostly empty, all the seniors left out of the senior trip are ushered into library for the day, which makes for an interesting motley crew of outsiders—all of us who didn't bother to order our high school yearbooks. The three girlfriends are now within glaring distance, as are their mean-looking Latino boyfriends. We've got the heavy-set girl who doesn't open her mouth for anybody and the kid with the tattoos all over his arms and the scrawny kid who gets picked on for no reason except that he's the scrawny kid. And over at our little corner is Trini. Great. All the school's bullies and targets together in one room. I'm feeling like I'm floating down the sewer with all the detritus of the school halls—the kids I never run into in a classroom because they're tracked in the remedial classes.

Since a number of the teachers (like Hotter, Doze and Melons) went along to the water park to chaperone, we get the reigning champ of good times to watch over the rest of us: Mr. Gump.

"Sit down! Be quiet! No sleeping!" Grump yells out whenever anyone even moves. His two-word commands get annoying after five minutes.

One of the Latino guys raises his hand.

"What is it?" Grump says, looking over his newspaper.

"Are we going to do anything else besides sit here all day?"

"You can read a book. You can do your homework," Grump offers.

Trini rolls her eyes. "Right." She pulls out a fashion magazine out of her handbag and starts to leaf through it.

Gump sees his long-time nemesis trying to defy his instructions and this time he's ready to battle. He walks over to Trini and this seems to catch every student's attention since everyone's bored and this looks like guaranteed drama. "I meant, read a book without pictures," he tells her.

"Well, *specify*," she says, wobbling her head.

"Ooh..." a guy in the back says. "You're going let the faggot talk to you like that, Gumpy?"

I was just about to say, *What is this? High school?* And then I realize that it is.

"Her name's Trini, guy. And that's Mr. Gump," Sebastián says, craning his neck over his shoulder. Although I can appreciate that chivalry is not dead, this gesture can only get him into trouble.

"I'm not talking to you, rich white boy ass-kisser," the guy shoots back.

"He's Argentinean-Italian-Mexican," I say, sounding particularly effeminate.

This incites an outburst from the tough kids. "Another faggot," he says. "Is that the faggot table?"

Mr. Gump spins on his heels and yells out, "Quiet! I'm not going to tolerate that kind of language around here! What's your name?"

"Danny Mayas," he replies.

"Well, Mr. My-ass," Grump says, and the room bursts open with laughter again. Even Trini can't help it.

Mr. Gump reaches his breaking point rather quickly and calls for back-up, and soon we've got Mr. Beasley to keep us company as well. He stares us all down like we're cut from the same loser cloth, and makes us all sit and pretend to read until lunch hour.

"Now I wish I were throwing myself down a water slide," I say as we sit sharing Sebastián's assortment of tin-canister lunch.

"I swear," says Trini. "They should institute the velvet rope policy in such places. I mean, since when does first class have to contend with the gripes and groans of coach?"

"You know, Maui," Sebastián says as he slurps a lo-mein noodle. "There's nothing wrong with standing up to such jerks."

"Yeah, Maui," Trini adds. "Thanks for sitting on your hands."

"I'm not going to antagonize those guys and get my ass kicked," I say. "And it's easy for you to say, Sebastián, you're taller and stronger."

"I'm not afraid of them," Trini says. "And I'm smaller than you."

"That's because you're a trannie," I say. "You girls are fierce fighters. I'm just your average gay boy who likes his face just the way it is."

At the use of the word *average* I feel something caught in my throat. But it's the truth. I don't like trouble. Does that make me a coward? Does that make me weak? It's called survival.

But the thought of having my best friend and my boyfriend think that about me makes me boil. "So what do you want me to do? Go in there and drop-kick Danny My-ass?"

"Forget it, Maui," Sebastián says. "I didn't mean to upset you."

"Well, you did," I say. "I can defend myself, I'm sure. If it comes to that. But unless I've got some gangster coming at me with a knife, I'm not sure I have to prove anything to him or to either of you."

"I said, forget about it," Sebastián says again.

"Save your karate chops for later, buddy," Trini says in a mock gruff voice. "We're heading back to the slammer."

Everyone takes their places again, but this time Mr. Beasley's not in the library, so this gives the tough guys permission to act up again as soon as we're seated.

"Enjoy your tea time, ladies?" Danny My-ass whispers from the next table.

I roll my eyes. But Trini, not one to resist talking back, goes for it.

"Enjoy your glue sniffing, homie?"

"Watch yourself, freak," Danny says. "I'll snap you in half with one hand."

"Try it and you lose your girlfriend, I mean, your hand," Sebastián says.

"You stay out of it, whitey," Danny says. He turns to point his finger at Trini. "And you've been warned, queer. Any more lip out of you and you're done."

"Mr. Gump," Trini says in her queeniest voice. "This young man here is making unsolicited advances on my person. Which encyclopedia book should I whack the shit out of him with? D for Don't-dick-me-unless-you-lick-me, Dildo? Or M for Make-a-move-and-I'll-man-rape-you, My-ass?"

It takes a minute for the whole of the insult to sink in, but when it does, everything happens at once: Danny lunges toward Trini, Sebastián lunges toward Danny, and Mr. Gump lunges for the telephone. The noise in the room runs its course from initial shock and awe, to rowdy cheering, to a screeching when suddenly the scuffle goes from a live-wire knot of arms and legs to bloodshed. Not even the three girlfriends approve of it and start to yell at Danny to back down. The girl who had the stare down with Trini comes over and casually squeezes her mace, which sends everyone on an immediate coughing and gagging fit.

The entire time I'm paralyzed. Is this the way I'm going to survive? By freezing? The playing dead tactic works on bears, I hear. Maybe it also works on assailants.

When security arrives we're already slumped all over the entrance to the library, Mr. Gump talks through a handkerchief over his face and points out the perpetrators: Danny, Trini and Sebastián.

"Wait," I tell Mr. Beasley between coughing fits. Tears are pouring out of the corners of my eyes. "You don't understand."

"Stand back and stay quiet, Mr. Gutiérrez, you'll hurt yourself," he says.

I watch helplessly as Sebastián and Danny are walked away with bloody faces and Trini has to be carried away in one of the security guard's arms.

"Whoever you are," Trini says in her Southern Belle accent. "I have always depended on the kindness of strangers." She waves at me over the man's shoulders.

"Mr. Beasley," I say. "Mr. Beasley, please, listen to me."

Mr. Beasley holds his hand up. "No, you listen to me. I'm tired of you kids causing problems here. Now, since we're on the final weeks of classes it defeats the purpose to give anyone detention, but I think I know what an appropriate punishment will be." He starts to direct the students to another building. "Get these kids some water, for crying out loud," he says.

I spend the rest of the time wondering if Trini and Sebastián are okay, but I don't have to figure out what Boozely was referring to: the prom.

At the end of the school day, Mr. Sandoval and Mr. Ramos are joined at the hip once again and come over together from the construction site to meet with the school principal. And when they all walk out of the administration office, I see two men wearing proud faces and two young men wearing angry ones. Since it's not a good idea for me to get in the way of that unhappy parade, I decide to make a few phone calls from my father's office at Las Cazuelas later that afternoon.

Sure enough, Mr. Beasley was just waiting for one of us to screw up so that he could save himself the trouble of having to deal with the Mariposa Club at the senior prom. Trini is beside herself with grief on the phone.

"Now I'll never get to debut my gown," she says, the final words of her sentences get drowned in an exaggerated moan.

"I don't understand," I say. "Your father looked very happy."

"Well, that's why. Because Boozely told him I couldn't go to the prom and wear my gown!"

"Oh. And what about Sebastián?"

"That's a whole other story. Mr. Sandoval sweet-talked Boozely into letting his son keep his squeaky-clean record since he was only jumping in to my defense."

"That's Mr. Sandoval," I say.

"And no one will ever see my gown!"

"Calm down, Trini, we'll figure something out. Let me call Sebastián and I'll call you later tonight."

I hang up and dial Sebastián. I only have ten minutes before I'm supposed to be out there directing people to their tables. But I figure Yolanda can hold down the fort until I get there.

"What's up, Maui?" Sebastián says.

"Sebastián, are you all right?" I ask.

"No big deal. It was mostly Danny's blood. I think Trini scratched the shit out of his face before I even got to him. How is she?"

"She's fine. A sprained knee. But what's really hurting her is that she lost her prom privileges."

"I know. Mr. Ramos could have bargained on her behalf the way my father did for me, but he seemed to be pleased by it. Mr. Beasley told him Trini was planning to wear a dress."

"It just seems like too severe a penalty. You know Boozely's just doing it to keep Trini from making a spectacle of the whole celebration."

"I know."

"Okay, and what do you think we should do about it?"

"What *can* we do, Maui? Call the ACLU? The Chicano Power group from the community college? We have no recourse here."

"Now, who's the coward?" I say.

"Okay, then what do *you* suggest?"

And I honestly don't know what to say. I wish Lib were here. He's the one with the mind for these kinds of things, but he's not coming back until tomorrow, and I won't see him at school until Wednesday.

"Maui?" Sebastián says.

"I have to get to work, Sebastián, I'll see you tomorrow in class." I hang up the phone.

My father comes in just as I stand up behind his desk.

"Maui," he says. "I didn't know you were in here."

"I had to check up on Trini and Sebastián. There was an incident in school today and they sort of got hurt."

He makes his concerned-father face. "Are they all right? Are *you* all right?"

"Yes," I say. "Except that Trini's paying a high price for it. I don't think it's fair."

"And Mr. Ramos?" he says, though I think he knows very well that it's a useless door to knock on. I simply shake my head.

I switch places with my father, but before I exit his office I decide to tap into his sensibilities once more.

"Papi," I say. He looks back at me. "If I were more like Trini, you know, more feminine and with an affinity for women's clothing, would you still love me?"

He seems slightly offended if not surprised by my question. "Maui, you and Mickey are all I have. I would love you and celebrate you regardless of how you talked or how you liked to dress."

"Thank you," I say and give him a hug. I head out to the locker room to put on my guayabera. This is just another night of gay hateration in good old Caliente. But there's love for us here as well.

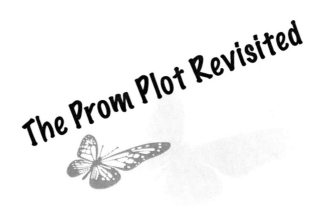

The Prom Plot Revisited

When Lib comes back to school on Wednesday, there's plenty to catch up on. Lib gushes when he describes the beauty of the Dartmouth campus and how there's this elaborate mural by Orozco in the college museum that just took his breath away. There's a business strip with cute little shops, quaint little restaurants and happening little bars, all within spitting distance of student housing, and, most importantly, to quote Lady Gaga: "Boys, boys, boys."

"There was so much eye candy up there I came back with cavities, girls," he says.

Trini yawns. "I don't understand why you have to fly all the way across country to look at boys. There's one sitting right here." She points at Sebastián.

"True," says Lib. "But there's also the small matter of my Ivy League education to consider. Not to mention I don't see anyone inviting you over to their campus. But don't worry, maybe you'll get lucky and the community college will mail you a bus pass."

"That's harsh, Lib," I say.

"Well, why does she always have to cop a squat over my dessert to piss? Why can't she be happy for me at least once?"

"Trini?" I say.

"Oh, all right," Trini says, throwing her arms up. "I'm sorry, Lib. I'm sorry about being Shady Lady about your wonderful trip. I guess I'm just a tad jealous that you get to go away to some glamorous town and all I've got is a shed behind Aunt Carmen's house. Give me a hug, you Goth teddy bear, and let me celebrate, not deprecate your big move to Bend-over."

"It's Hanover," Lib says. "But let's hope I get some of that as well."

Sebastián applauds. "See? That wasn't too bad now, was it?"

"So what did I miss while I was gone?" Lib says.

We fill him in on the rumble that cost Trini her prom ticket, which sends Trini digging through her purse for a tissue. Sebastián mentions how Mr. Sandoval had negotiated not to revoke those privileges, and how Mr. Ramos stepped in and decided that this was an appropriate punishment for his son, who should know better than to fight in school.

"It was so humiliating," Trini says, sobbing. "Like anyone didn't know that the real lesson I was being taught was not to cross-dress."

"So we're tossing around some options, Lib, but none that would actually work," I say. "We could use your brain right about now."

Lib scratches his head. "Well, let me think on it and let's reconvene at lunch. We might be able to get away with something yet."

So on that note, we head out to mull our way through first period, then second, then study hour, until we're back together again at the Queer Planter for lunch hour.

"Maybe we can get an outside group involved," I say. "Like one of the LGBT organizations that gave you a scholarship, Lib."

Lib shakes his head. "I would, except that it's going to be so easy for Mr. Beasley to hide behind his policies. In the end, Trini *is* being punished for inciting violence."

"You can't blame the victim," Trini says.

"I'm not," Lib says. "I'm just saying that since Danny What's-his-name also got *his* prom privileges revoked, well, then, it doesn't appear that Trini's being singled out."

"What about the media?" Trini says. "Lib, you've got connections there, can't you call one of those TV crews over and have them do an exposé?" She slips into an anchor voice: "*Teenage cross-dressers and the principals who hate them. Film at eleven.*"

"Maybe," Lib says. "Though there's got to be a newsworthy angle to it other than Trini not being able to showcase her gown."

"That's it," Sebastián says.

"What's it?" I say.

"Trini's gown."

"I still don't follow you, Sebastián, what about the gown?" I say.

Sebastián launches into his explanation: "Trini's gown is the true symbol of our protest, right? So it really doesn't matter who wears it as long as it makes its way to the prom."

"I'm lost," Trini says. "You want to show up with my gown as your date?"

"Brilliant!" Lib says. "Sebastián is right. Trini has been banned from the prom, but not her gown. So all we have to do is find someone else who can go to the prom wearing it. We'd still be able to enter the prom court since Sebastián is Prom Prince. All we need is a new Prom Princess."

All three of them look at me. "What?" I say, jumping to my feet. "No way!"

"It makes sense, Maui," Lib says. "I'd be more than happy to wear it but I wouldn't be able to fit my leg through it."

"Not to mention it's not your color," Trini adds. Lib pouts.

"Come on, Maui," Sebastián says. "This is your chance, a chance for the Mariposa Club."

"I agree, Passion Flower, you've already got your drag name," Trini says. "I think you would look gorgeous in my gown. Not as great as me, of course, I mean, look at that neck of yours, but you're close enough."

"No," I say, stepping away from the three of them as if they're trying to force me into the gown that very second.

"You can't say no," Trini says. "The very idea that my gown will make its debut after all gives me chills!"

"No, no, no," I say. I've never worn a dress, and despite that hypothetical question that I posed to my father in his office, I have no desire to start now. No, no, no, no, no. That's the end of it. No way, no how, no.

On Saturday, Sebastián drives me to the Glamorous Grotto for a fitting.

Passion Flower

How to describe wearing a dress? Maybe my boy upbringing has spoiled me but I like the feeling of having legs. With a piece of fabric constricting my body's most basic movements, I can't even begin to imagine how women who wear these thigh straitjackets are able to get anywhere without punch-kissing the floor every two feet. Even with my slim torso I still have to suck in my stomach for Trini to force the zipper up my spine, and suddenly the blood in my arms can't circulate. The other deceptive thing about this gown is that it's heavy. I feel as if I'm wearing a drape lined with stones. So Virginia Woolf.

"Geez, Trini, how can you keep your back straight in this thing, it keeps pulling me down," I complain.

"Just pose as if you're looking down from an incline," Trini says. "That's it."

"I'm going to tip over," I say.

"Okay, not too far back, you're bringing out your *chorizo con huevos*," she says.

I fold my body back in and put my hands over my crotch.

Trini's eyes widen. "Oh, honey, you're like seventeen years old and your boobs are already sagging. Yowzah, what happened to the left one?"

Sebastián laughs from the divan.

I look at him. "Don't, or I'll make *you* wear it!"

"I think you look great," Sebastián says. "Flattering to your girlish figure."

"Okay," Trini says. "Now take a few steps, but don't fall because if you rip it that's the end of the gown."

I wobble a few steps and after a few uncertain minutes, I gain some confidence and begin to strut.

"Sweetie," Trini says. "You're walking like a Mexico City whore. Keep your knees together."

Sebastián gets up and stands next to me and offers me his arm. I hold on to his elbow and start to learn how to walk like a lady.

"That's it," Trini says. "Keep the hymen intact."

After a few more strolls inside the Glamorous Grotto without losing my balance, Trini springs the bad news: "Okay, now let's try that with heels on."

"You're kidding me," I say.

How can women put their own shoes on while wearing a dress? Or do they put their shoes on first and then slip the dress on? Who knew I'd be asking myself these questions?

The shoes are a bit too small for me, so Sebastián agrees to buy me a pair.

"And *you* know how to pick a nice pair of hoof bling?" Trini asks.

"I've accompanied my mother to Rodeo Drive on many an occasion," he says. "I know women's shoes."

In the meantime, we make do with Trini's. It's like going back to square one. I'll have to ask Mickey when I get home how many times has she twisted her ankle on a pair of these elevated babies?

And how many times have her calves cramped? Mine, about twice so far.

An hour later, I need a long break, so I change into my shorts and Sebastián massages my legs while Trini works on cleaning up my eyebrows and picking out my makeup.

"I could get used to this pampering," I say. "If only I didn't have to suffer so much just to get here."

"My goodness, Maui," Trini says. "You have no eyeliner build-up whatsoever, and you've been skipping out on your electrolysis sessions, haven't you. I'm going to knit a wristband with these thick eyebrow hairs of yours."

"Don't over-pluck, Trini," I say. "This is only for one night."

After a few painful plucks, she wipes off my face with a damp towel, and then starts to experiment on the eye shadow.

"With your olive, watered-down glass of chocolate milk complexion," Trini says, applying the first strokes. "I'd say a courageous tone of gray to pick up the accents on the gown. Maybe I'll outline it nice and thick to make it reach out and scratch the competition's eyes out."

"I'm going to scratch my own eyes out if this itching doesn't stop," I say.

"Wait until we get to the wig, and then you'll really know what itching means."

"Nice," Sebastián says.

"Wig? I don't remember you wearing a wig when you wore this gown?"

"That's because it wasn't ready, but I've been working on a special number just for you, Passion Flower."

"How do you subject yourself to this torture, Trini?" I say.

"No pain, no gain," she says.

Maybe another hour goes by, I'm not sure. I lose all perspective of time while under the full-identity makeover of Trinidad Ramos. The longer I'm inside this new me, the more comfortable

I feel, the more natural it becomes to walk on my toes, swivel my hips, and make graceful circles in the air with my shoulders.

The wig isn't so bad except that it's prickly and the bangs keep poking my eyes. The hair comes down over my ears, but Trini still insists on clip-on earrings, in case I decide to pull back my hair and wear a flower or something.

"The only drawback is that you perspire so much," says Trini. "And we need to do something about these panty lines. They're so unbecoming. Would you be opposed to a cake-cutting thong?"

"I would," I say.

Sebastián takes a look at my butt. "Or maybe a jockstrap would help."

"Don't encourage her," I say.

Trini manages the entire transformation like a true pro. She steps back, puts her hand on her hip, steps forward again and makes an adjustment here and there. And when it's all complete, she makes her final assessment: "Well, we have about two weeks before prom, so I think we can iron out the details by then. But next Saturday, you're all mine again."

"Now what?" I say.

"Now you take everything off," Trini says. "Shouldn't take more than another hour."

How do women do this? How does *anyone*?

Trini throws us out of the Glamorous Grotto because she's got "work to do," and I happily step out of the warm and claustrophobic shed with Sebastián, since we're now on to the next stage of the game. We get in the Saab and head downtown.

Here's another advantage for boys: Such chores as picking out a tux are fast and easy. We select a number in charcoal and Sebastián then stands there with his arms out, getting his measurements taken, and within half an hour, we're done with the tuxedo rental place. It's a good thing anyway, since we don't have that much time to hang around tonight. We need to pick Lib up at Las Cazuelas and give him a ride home.

"That was rather anti-climactic," I say as we head out the door and all Sebastián has to carry is a tiny slip of paper in his hand.

"What do you mean? I still have to come back and pick up the tux, and then drop it off when I'm done with it. That's a lot of mileage," he says, smiling coyly.

Since we're in the area, I decide to do a little graduation gift-shopping for Lib and Trini. I want something simple, not too expensive. Maybe a lady's scarf for Trini's neck and some schmancy cloth for Lib's Gothic ballerina creations, so we walk into an accessory boutique, where everything looks so delicate, so dainty and shiny it makes me worry I'll sneeze and knock something over. We're the only customers in the store. Sebastián's iPhone rings, which is rare since he doesn't get many calls, except from Mr. Sandoval.

"It's my mom," he says. "Do you mind browsing on your own while I take this? It might be a while."

"That's fine," I say, and he walks out of the boutique to take the call.

I'm absent-mindedly fingering some of the scarves and trying to imagine Trini (or the Gothic ballerinas) prancing around in the prints, when I get the sensation that I'm being watched. I turn my head. The young woman behind the counter keeps a steady eye on me. At first I'm indignant, thinking that she probably suspects I came in here to shoplift, but when I see past the blouse and jacket, I recognize my observer: it's the mace-wielding Latina from school, except she doesn't have as much eye makeup on today. Great, I say. Now I'm on her turf. The only consolation I have is that she works here, so I doubt she'll be unprofessional and verbally assault me or something.

"Hello," she says. "Let me know if I can help you with anything."

Good. She's keeping it on the down-low. "Thank you, I'm fine," I say.

I want to browse for at least another minute before I bolt so that I don't let her think she scared me away. Or even better, I'm hoping Sebastián will come back in and that way we will outnumber her two-to-one. Listen to me, why am I frightened? And then my nerves really get rattled when she steps around the counter and walks up to me.

"There's a sale on scarves this week," she says.

I swallow hard. "Thank you," I say. *Now, go away!*

"And over here," she says, pulling a shawl off its display. "We've got these, which are also on sale. You're buying a gift for your mother?"

"For a friend," I say. "She likes these kinds of things."

"Go ahead, feel it," she says.

I reach out to touch the shawl but my palm is sweaty. I don't know what kind of head game she's playing but it's making me nauseous. And why does she look so familiar? That's when it hits me. It hits me so hard I want to go through the wall. Her name tag confirms it. This young woman is Amanda, Tony Sánchez's girlfriend—*the* Tony Sánchez, who attacked Lib and killed himself at the mall last year. She looks even prettier than the picture he showed me when we were sitting together at the bus stop. But I can't read her emotions. Is she angry at me? Is she sad for me? I don't know.

"Thank you, I, I think I'm going to look somewhere else," I stutter, out of breath.

"Are you all right?" she asks. "Can I get you some water?"

"No," I say. But I'm feeling light-headed. Maybe it was sucking in my stomach and walking around on the balls of my feet all those hours at Trini's that has finally caught up to me, but I need to sit down.

Amanda walks me by the elbow to a chair next to the counter, and when I get my bearings back I decide to come clean.

"I know who you are," I say.

"And I know who *you* are," she says. "We go to the same high school."

"I meant, you're Tony Sánchez's girl. Or were."

Amanda smiles. "No, Maui, that's just something I let him say to protect himself. We weren't that kind of couple, just very good friends. But nobody needed to know, certainly no one from Los Calis."

"I'm very sorry about what happened to him," I say. My mind zips back to the afternoon at the mall with the gang members threatening Lib. I'm more relaxed now that I know she's not plotting a revenge killing.

"I'm sorry too."

I have the urge to hug her, but it's all happening so quickly, this chance encounter with a flash from my past.

"You know he liked you, didn't you?" she says.

I feel my neck growing warm. Maybe I don't need to hear this.

"But he liked a lot of boys. And it pained him that none of them liked him back. It was hard for him, you know."

"I know," I say. And there's nothing more I *can* say. We simply allow our thoughts and memories to collide inside our heads as the we soak in the silence.

At this point, we're both teary-eyed, so Amanda walks back to the counter and searches for a tissue in her purse. She hands me one and I take it.

"Thank you," I say.

She smiles and lets out a laugh. "I think Tony would have found this amusing."

I smile back and I let Amanda slip into a brief but touching monologue about this boy we both knew.

When the boutique door opens again, Sebastián walks in and looks surprised to see me sitting down.

"Hey," he says. "Everything all right?"

I nod. "I think we should head out now. By the way, this is Amanda. She goes to school with us."

Sebastián extends his hand. "Nice to meet you," he says, without realizing that they've crossed paths before, that this isn't the first time she has made me cry.

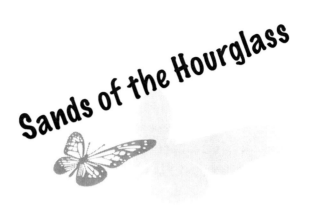

Sands of the Hourglass

The following week slips through our fingers with no further dramas, at least not with the seniors. We hear about fights and turf battles concerning the underclassmen but these are of no interest to those of us who are rapidly distancing our psyches from those letters stitched to our bodies, à la Hester Prynne, these last four years: CVHS—Caliente Valley High School.

Since the baby-ballooning Mrs. Ramos has been spending more time at home with Aunt Carmen, Trini has been taking advantage of her free time to explore the fashion opportunities available to her in Palm Springs. Her charm even got her an impromptu interview at a clothing boutique owned by an older gay couple who were pleased to know that fierce flamership was alive and well in the next generation.

Sebastián and I have been seeing less of each other between schooldays, only because Mr. Sandoval has been demanding more quality time with his son, who will move across the country right after graduation. He even put his budding romance with

Yolanda on the back burner, but she's fine with that since she knows Mr. Sandoval will be all hers as soon as Sebastián is out of the picture.

Sandra and Mickey are on better terms though Sandra hasn't changed her mind about staying in Caliente for another year; Maddy, the other pregnant woman in my immediate circle of acquaintances, is just about to burst open to let Robbie breathe on his (or her) own; and Isaac, believe it or not, sent me an email wishing me and the girls a fabulous mariposa graduation.

There was so much I wanted to talk to Isaac about since he can't even begin to imagine the plot twists and life turns that we've experienced these last few months, and I'm sure he's got plenty of his own, but in the end I simply thanked him and wished him luck in whatever he was up to in LA. He did mention that he had seen Mr. Dutton, and that they were on better terms, and that made me happy. I didn't ask him any questions when I hit reply, though I was curious to know if he was still with Armando. I figured this was a one-time exchange, not the beginning of a back-and-forth dialogue. Otherwise, he would have called.

Lib has been keeping to himself most of all because he's feverishly writing the perfect valedictorian speech. Even at the Mexican curio market I catch him pouring over his notes, scratching words out on the page and sucking on the top of his pen as he reflects on what he was already written. I asked for a preview but permission was denied: it's a surprise.

Eight days to prom night, Trini picks me up for our finishing touches and lessons on prom gown decorum. But before I rush out the door because Paulina Rubio is honking outside, Mickey stops me.

"Maui, where are you going?"

"I've got plans with Trini," I tell her. "It's my day off, remember?"

"I know it's your day off, I just thought—" She doesn't finish her sentence.

My expression softens. "Is it Sandra?"

She shakes her head. "Maui, you know what day it is?"

"Saturday."

"Maui," she says, exasperated. "It's Mami's birthday. Don't you want to come with me to take her flowers?"

Paulina Rubio keeps honking. Good grief, I completely forgot, and the guilt comes crashing down on me.

"I really have to do this," I say. "It's kind of important, but if you wait for me I can be back in a few hours. Or you can pick me up at Trini's."

"I can do that," she says. "I don't want to go by myself. Three o'clock?"

"Three o'clock."

I throw open the front door. "Trini! I'm getting there!" I turn back to look at my sister. We have so much in common Mickey and I. We even have the same sensitive souls.

The few hours I spend with Trini are light-hearted and fun. Though on one occasion Mr. Ramos comes knocking on the door to tell Trini that he's taking Mrs. Ramos to pre-natal care and Trini should check in on Aunt Carmen once in a while. I'm hiding behind the door with my gown half-way up my torso, but Mr. Ramos would never bother coming in, so I have nothing to fear.

"All these pregnant women around us," Trini says. "What do the rest of us do with our baby batter but smear it on paper tissue before we toss it."

"That's gross." I wince. But she's right. That's exactly what I do with mine.

At three o'clock Mickey comes by and I say goodbye to Trini, who hands me a small paper flower with glitter on it.

"Put this on Mrs. Gutiérrez's grave for me," she says. I give her a hug and climb into Mickey's car.

We don't talk on the way to the cemetery. It's a time for reflection. A sadness comes over me. Mami won't get to see me graduate from high school. She won't get to see me graduate from college. There are many ceremonies we won't get to share, except for this one—my yearly visit to her grave on her birthday. We used to come more often in the beginning: on the anniversary of her death, on Mothers Day, and around all the major holidays, but Papi decided that it was too unhealthy, that we weren't allowing ourselves to heal by breaking down into tears each time we stood at the grave and were reminded of the huge loss we had suffered. So we decided to narrow it down to one visit. Papi comes on his own, on the anniversary of their marriage, which is sometime in July. He doesn't mention what he does or what he says. It's his own private grief. And this is Mickey's and mine.

We pull into the parking lot, and then walk through the main path. Mickey's got a small bouquet of flowers, I just have Trini's little paper flower in my hand. There are a few other mourners scattered about, but mostly this cemetery is all headstones, a few mausoleums and wreaths in various stages of decay. A groundskeeper stands in the distance with one hand on a rake while another brings a cigarette to his mouth.

I suppose cemeteries are quiet because most of the talking takes place inside the head. And whatever complaints or confessions any of these people have they keep buried in their coffins. We come up to Mami's grave: ADELITA GUTIÉRREZ: BELOVED WIFE AND MOTHER. Dead five years.

Mickey puts her offering down first. And then I do. We keep our silence for an extended period, usually until one of us breaks it. Today, Mickey does the honors.

"It feels so strange, doesn't it, that we're leaving Caliente behind? We've been here all of our lives."

“Yeah,” I respond. “But we get to take some good memories with us.”

“And a few bad ones. But that’s how it usually goes.”

After another extended silence, I speak up: “Do you think Papi will be okay once we leave?”

Mickey runs her hands through her hair. “I’ve been thinking about that, but we’ll be close enough that we can drive down when we need to if he gets lonely. But who knows, maybe he’ll find someone. Look at Mr. Sandoval.”

“Geez, does everyone know about Yolanda?”

“Yes. *Because* of Yolanda. She’s been broadcasting it all over the place.”

I giggle. I can totally picture that.

“How about you and Sebastián Sandoval?” Mickey asks.

We’re both looking out into the expanse of resting places. But it doesn’t seem disrespectful to talk about love or relationships since we’re doing what all of the deceased probably wish they were doing: living.

“We’re keeping it cool,” I say. “Whatever we have is not going to move past graduation. It’s easier if we simply stay friends. You know how it is.”

“Yes,” Mickey says. “I know. Sandra and I have decided on the same thing.”

It takes me a moment to wrap my brain around the implications of what my sister just said. Did I hear that right? She and Sandra? My sister…couldn’t be! I turn to look at her.

“For a second there I thought you were telling me that you and Sandra were like girlfriend and girlfriend.”

Mickey turns her head to face me.

“Oh, my God,” I say. “You’re a lesbian? But I thought you liked boys?”

Mickey laughs. "Gosh, Maui, you and your labels. Sexuality is complex, you know. I do like boys, and on occasion I fall for a girl. Nothing out of this world."

Knock me over with a boa feather! Well, it makes sense why she was particularly hurt by Sandra's political actions. And all those fights and tears. But then I feel a little bit cheated.

"Why didn't you tell me this before?" I say.

"Because, Maui, I was confused by the whole thing. Not being in love with a girl, but being in love with Sandra. I needed to sort things out before I could tell anybody. Besides, I thought that you of all people had figured that one out a long time ago. These feelings are not new to me, but talking about them is. So be nice."

We turn back toward the open cemetery and let the exchange sink in.

After another pause, I ask: "Are you going to tell Papi?"

"I'm not ready," she says. " And I don't know what's going to happen next, when we get to Riverside. Maybe I'll fall in love with a boy and there will be no need to tell him anything. But if I fall in love with a girl, then that's a different story. I'll cross that bridge when I get there."

"Don't worry. Your secret's safe with me."

As we stand there, a woman passes behind us. The scent of a familiar perfume awakens my nose. It's the same perfume Mami used to wear, I'd recognize it anywhere. Mickey's probably thinking the same thing because she too does a double take as the woman turns at a mausoleum and then vanishes. I think it's a sign of approval. I'll go ahead and believe that. I'm not saying it was Mami's ghost or anything like that. I'm just saying it was the spirit world's way of sending a message: *Don't worry about it. Just keep on living.*

Soon after, we leave the cemetery. I'm hungry, so Mickey offers to buy me dinner. It's been a while since we've had a meal together, just the two of us, brother and sister. And I suspect that her revelation that afternoon is the ultimate offering of trust since we'll continue living together in the fall, but under very different circumstances. I'm comforted by this. We have broken out of our childhood cocoons.

A Walk in the Clouds

The big night finally arrives and I'm so nervous about going out in public in drag that I spend more time than I want to on the porcelain throne. My sweat glands are like on steroids and keep pumping out the cries for help. And the butterflies in my stomach have migrated north and are now all locked up inside my heart and hating it.

"Relax, already," Trini says, "I'm trying to color in the eyebrows evenly. You want to look like Harry Potter and have lightning shapes on your face?"

"I'm *trying*," I say.

Lib is wearing a rather arresting Goth garb in maroon and black that makes him look like he's been snatched away from the Victorian era. He stands, fumbling around with the camera. Since Trini can't go in, she demands plenty of photographs of the big event. My date has yet to show up with my shoes, so I'm worried that I'll have to wear Trini's tiny toe-crunchers.

“I’m not sure how good the pictures will come out,” Lib says. “It might depend on the lighting. Plus, I hear that they’ve got these smoke machines from hell set up.”

“Smoke machines?” Trini says. “How tacky. What’s the theme? California Wildfires?”

Lib stands up and makes an arc with one of his hands. “A Walk in the Clouds. I bet the prom committee gave the pharmaceutical company some good business. I hear it’s all cotton and gauze.”

“Well, I suppose that’s not a bad idea in case this one falls on his face and starts to bleed,” Trini says. “He can just reach over and apply first-aid on himself.”

“Not funny.” I say.

“I wish you had let Sebastián rent the limo, Maui,” Lib says. He walks over to one of the Glamorous Grotto’s many mirrors and reapplies his black lipstick. “I’ve never been in one.”

“I know,” I say as Trini starts putting on the wig. “I just didn’t want him to do all the spending. He bought our tickets, he’s buying the shoes. Ouch! Careful, Trini, my ear.”

Trini shrugs. “Sorry. They’re rather large, aren’t they?”

Lib takes a look. “Maybe a little uneven also. The left one’s kind of low on the side of the head. But the crooked nose draws attention away from it.”

“I hadn’t noticed that, but you’re right,” Trini says. “Maybe I can pull the hair up to the side like this and resurrect the right cheekbone, bring back some symmetry to the otherwise misshapen face.”

“Why don’t I just show up to the prom with a paper bag over my head?” I say.

Lib and Trini laugh. “We’re just kidding!” Trini says. “You’re perfect, Passion Flower. Just perfect.” She leans down and gives me a peck on the nose.

And then there’s a knock on the door. Trini puts her hand over her mouth. “Girl, your date’s here!”

Lib opens the door and Sebastián stands at the entrance with a corsage in a clear plastic box and my shoes. "*Entrée*," Lib says.

"Evening, ladies," Sebastián says. "How's my cross-dressing angel? Ready for a walk in the clouds?"

I want to throw myself at him. He's absolutely dreamy in his cute little silver vest and tie. His green eyes are as sharp as darts tonight and they pierce all of my erogenous zones at once. It's that hot.

"Can I come in?" he says.

The three of us react at once, realizing that we've just been staring at him. "Oh, yes, come in, by all means," Trini says.

"I brought the shoes," Sebastián says, holding them up.

"Wait, wait," Trini says. "I want all of this caught on camera. Lib?"

Lib does his best to keep up with the ceremonial slipping-on of the corsage. I blush like Cinderella when Sebastián kneels to slip the beautiful silver slippers on my non-pedicured feet. They're going to kill me tonight because they're not broken in, but, hey, Prince Charming bought them for me so I'm just going to grin and bear it.

We spend the next fifteen minutes posing and hamming it up for the camera, but too soon we have to get going and leave Trini behind, which stings a little. Trini takes it in stride. Of all of us, she's the true survivor.

"I promise to take as many pictures as I can. I have plenty of film," Lib says.

"I'll do your gown proud," I say.

"Give me a hug," Sebastián tells Trini and Trini flings herself against him.

"Thank you, my hunky Latin lover. I'll sleep with a pepper in my mouth tonight and think of you," she says.

"All righty, then," Lib says. "Let's get going!"

Fortunately, Mr. and Mrs. Ramos don't even bother poking their heads out of the window so they don't get to see me walk like a duck as my heels sink into the lawn. Sebastián, a gentleman to the end, opens the car doors for both Lib and me, and then we're off to the high school gym for A Walk in the Clouds.

I'm terrified about stepping out of the car when we park at the lot, but it's dark and everyone seems to be in a particularly generous mood so I hold my breath and allow Sebastián to help me out of my seat. The three of us walk up to the front door and no one bats an eye when Sebastián hands over the tickets and we step inside. It's Lib who gets all the second looks. That's when I realize that nobody recognizes me. They all actually think I'm a girl. This gives me courage to carry on without fear for the rest of the evening, even as we take a seat at a table with a cute couple I have seen around campus but have never met.

"Hi," the guy says.

"Hello," Sebastián says. "Nice set up."

The guy's date nods her head. Indeed it's not a bad production. I had this image of sloppy wall dressings and distorted cloud formations, but the prom committee went all out on the cardboard cut-outs and the stretched cotton that makes it look as if we're holding a party in heaven. Cherubs and cupids abound on the walls, dangling from the ceiling and even lying down at the center of each table. There's a smoke machine all right, but it's barely spitting out plumes that stay low to the ground and don't overrun the place like a Stephen King movie. Not bad at all.

The music's playing and the lights are low and blue, and I elbow Sebastián each time I see one of our teachers. Everyone's here—Hotter, Melons, even Mr. Knowles with a rather young and attractive Mrs. Knowles.

Mr. Beasley does his Class of 2011 thing and that gets everybody excited and after the compulsory speech about proper behavior and manners, he asks the DJ to start the dance.

Since it's a fast-paced number, I let Sebastián take Lib out to the dance floor and no one seems to care that it's two guys dancing together. I relax and take a sip of my water. When I set the water back on the table, I'm dismayed that I left most of my lipstick on the side of the plastic glass.

"I do that all the time," the girl at my table says. She pulls out a mirror for me.

That's when I realize that not only do I not have a purse, I didn't bring the lipstick. Be kind. It's my first night as a female.

"Thank you," I say and wave the mirror away.

"I'm Veronica," she says.

"I'm Maui," I say.

"Interesting name. Is it short for something?" she asks.

"Mauricio," I say. Oops.

She looks at me with shock and then she leans in to whisper into her date's ear. He looks at me closely, and when he too figures it out, he gets up and takes Veronica with him.

Nice. Batting zero and moving into the negative numbers.

When Lib and Sebastián come back I tell them what happened.

"I wouldn't worry about it," Sebastián says. "What's the worst they can do?"

We get our answer when Principal Beasley comes up to our table. He leans in to look at me.

"You couldn't leave well enough alone," he says. Lib takes out his camera and takes a picture. Boozely glares at him.

Sebastián steps in. "We paid for the prom tickets, Mr. Beasley. And the dress code said formal wear. You're looking at it."

Boozely rolls his eyes, shakes his head and throws his hands up in the air before he walks away.

"That wasn't too bad," Lib comments.

The next few dances take place without incident, though word is beginning to spread that there's a guy in drag sitting at table 5, which is now the pariah table because no one will join us. I lose the courage to go out to the dance floor because I'm too tense and am afraid I've unlearned all the tricks to drag balance. Still, this doesn't dampen the overall celebratory mood and eventually a few of the students come over to chat, either out of curiosity or out of generosity, it's never clear. But the tide turns and the graduating seniors are too busy having a good time to care. That is, until the prom court is asked to step up to the stage.

One thing is blending in with the crowd, and another is coming under the scrutiny of the student body that has been asked to cast its votes. Sebastián grabs my hand and takes me up to the stage. The laughter begins. At first it's just an isolated chuckle here and there but then when the rest of the group catches on it's a full-on laugh fest. I have this *Carrie* flashback moment and I feel like an idiot.

"Just relax," Sebastián tells me, but it's not him up here in a gown and shoes that are beginning to make my feet blister.

"Is this a joke?" another member of the prom court asks. Lib continues to take pictures.

Mr. Beasley and another teacher walk up to the front and beckon us off the stage, but Sebastián won't budge.

"I think we should listen to them," I plead.

"Mr. Sandoval, Mr. Gutiérrez," Mr. Beasley says. "Now!"

By this point, even the DJ has noticed the fuss and cranes his neck from behind his assortment of turntables and speakers. I hear shouts here and there saying, "Throw them out!" But then I also hear, "Let them stay!" Lib catches wind of this and begins the chant: "Let them stay! Let them stay! Let them stay!" The chant catches on and overpowers the nay-sayers.

"I told you to have faith," Sebastián says.

"Let them stay! Let them stay! Let them stay!"

Not everyone is happy, but it appears that it's easier to just move on than to let the tension escalate. Boozely throws his hands up in the air again and backs away. The prom committee emcee goes up on the stage to continue the ceremony.

"Okay, seniors, settle down," the emcee says. "Let's first give a round of applause to the prom court. Don't let it be said we discriminate here at CV High!" Cheering and hollering ensues.

"And now for the announcement of the Prom King and Queen..."

Lib crosses his fingers with one hand, takes pictures with the other.

"Ladies and gentlemen: King José Luis Martínez and Queen Lily Mendoza!"

Queen Lily in particular gushes with excitement as she's crowned with a small tiara that doesn't want to stay up on her head. Pictures are taken, though it's clear that the shot of the night is of me standing next to Sebastián.

"See?" Sebastián says. "It's not about actually winning the crown. It's about being allowed to be in the running."

Still, as the princes and princesses who didn't win step off the stage to allow the newly-crowned king and queen to have their first royal dance, I feel slightly disappointed.

"You guys looked great up there," someone says to us as we walk back to our table. "Good work, guys," someone else chimes in.

Lib, our one-person paparazzi, takes pictures all the way to the table. And just like that, the celebration continues and everyone's back on the dance floor. The Prom King and Queen just two more bodies in the crowd.

"I'd say we showed them," Lib says, nodding his head.

"Showed them what?" I say. "Do you think we really made a difference here? Are all of these people going to go away tonight with a more sensitive understanding of cross-dressers and gay people?"

Sebastián looks at me with pity. "So do you think we shouldn't have even made an effort? Should we not have bothered? Should we continue to be invisible?"

I blush. I guess I spoke too soon, still reeling from the anxiety of standing on the stage with a gown. At least no one dropped pig's blood on my head.

"No, I guess not, I—I'm just a little tense that's all."

"I think I have the cure for that," Sebastián says. He stands up and holds out his hand. "You owe me a dance."

I hesitate, but then put it in check. How much more can I draw attention to myself? I just stood up in front of everybody, wearing a homemade gown and an itchy wig. I get up and Sebastián leads me to the dance floor. It's a slow number, of course, and though I fumble at first about where to put my arms on my dance partner, I adapt quickly. When the dance floor opens up around us, I realize that Sebastián and I are being ostracized but also recognized for what we did tonight, even if all it meant for some of the students was one more unexpected element, one more thing to talk about when they remember their prom. I put my head against Sebastián's shoulder and for one brief moment, swaying among the angels and clouds, I feel like I'm in heaven.

But that moment too passes. And the party-goers are interested in more partying, more dancing, not in who was crowned or who showed up in a gown instead of a tux. I suppose that's the point to all of this: Live and let live.

The night winds down and I'm exhausted. Even sitting in a gown is work, so when it's time to leave there's another spurt of dirty looks and thumbs up, but we make our way back to the car without getting spat on or having to exchange insults.

"I didn't see Mr. Beasley anywhere," Sebastián says. "I wanted to say good night."

Lib chuckles. "Yeah, I'm sure he misses us too."

We drop Lib off and fifteen minutes later Sebastián and I are sitting in the driveway at my place. The house is unusually dark and quiet.

"I know Papi's probably still at the restaurant," I say. "But I wonder where Mickey's off to."

"Can we go inside for a minute?" Sebastián asks. "It might be more comfortable for both of us since you can hardly move in that dress."

I mull it over. Maybe this is like a prom night cliché but then, how many guys lose their virginity to another guy? I'm sure it happens. But it's probably not common. Maybe tonight's the night after all. Yes? No? Yes?

"All right," I say.

Sebastián gets out, opens the door for me. He takes my backpack out of the trunk and I dig for the keys, my hand a little shaky because I've made up my mind about something incredibly important. I give him a throat-tickling kiss before opening the door, and when it swings open, the living room lights go on and there's Mickey and Papi and a cake that reads: *CONGRADS!* with a *d*. Get it?

"Surprise!" they yell out. But the surprise seems to be on them. Jaws drop, eyes pop out, and I'm working hard to hide what's bulging out of my gown.

"Nice corsage," Mickey finally says.

My father remains speechless. Sebastián begins to chuckle, and I'm positive that we're going to stay up and eat cake and ice cream until it's time for Sebastián to go home.

I roll with it. "Would you believe this was the last clean outfit in the closet?"

Butterfly High

June graduation. Girls and Trini wear velvet red; the boys wear royal blue, our school colors. And while everyone's taking their places, no one's having as good of a time as Trini with the twirling tassel on the cap's mortarboard. We go through one boring rehearsal the afternoon before and now we're sitting there in garbs that don't breathe very well, on uncomfortable seats sinking into the lawn of the athletic field, with all of our friends and relatives on the hard, butt-numbing bleachers. But we're all here, going though another rite of passage together. We stand for the Pledge of Allegiance, someone sings the school fight song, and Principal Beasley presides over this and that as each member of the distinguished group on the stage takes a turn at the microphone. Since the rest of us are seated in alphabetical order, I'm far away from Sebastián and Trini, and I wish I were as lucky as the person sitting next to me, who's texting away with someone in the back.

I go into my daze, like many others, I'm sure, until it's time for Lib to deliver his valedictorian speech at the podium. We applaud, there's a bit of feedback when Lib says good evening, and though he looks a little nervous up there at first, he eventually hits his stride. Let's listen in:

> Esteemed faculty, fellow graduates, beloved friends and family, I stand up here this evening not as the best student of the class of 2011, but as the representative of a group that today says goodbye to its last childhood cradle and moves into the uncertain but wondrous world of adulthood.
>
> We must be grateful for the life lessons taught to us by our teachers and guardians. They have prepared us with the wisdom and insights to make informed decisions, to rejoice in our successes and reflect on our shortcomings, and to express our emotions, prejudices and discontents with constructive language and tolerance. You see, we occupy a place of individual responsibility, where what we say and what we do carries the weight of consequence. Every one of us is a drop in the lake that will ripple. Every one of us must choose the kind of positive or negative energy to unleash on our community.
>
> We have experienced plenty of the ugly energies: from the unfortunate death of our beloved cohort, Antonio Sánchez, to the verbal and physical attacks on our gay and transgender youth. But so too have we seen moments of enlightenment, like the founding of our high school's first LGBT organization, and the unhindered reception of the first same-sex couple at the senior prom.

There's an uncomfortable tension in the air and Principal Beasley shifts in his seat as if he wants to leap up and put a stop to Lib's speech, but he doesn't. There a few isolated boos from the crowd, but not enough to cause alarm.

> I know that this might frighten some and make others nervous, and I will not judge you or silence you. But so too do I expect not to be judged or silenced in return.

A supportive applause breaks out from different directions, and this makes me breathe a little easier. It's going to be all right.

> Let us celebrate, not deprecate those who will not only dare to dream of a better world, but take action to achieve it. If high school is the place that opens our eyes to possibility and potential, then it is a good place to have called our home.
>
> Parents and family members, thank you for nurturing us. Faculty, thank you for maturing us. Friends, thank you for the banter, the jokes, the tears, the laughs, the fights and the reconciliations—every exchange is a testament to the most precious and valuable relationships we will ever know.
>
> *Quisiera también agradecerles a mis padres su apoyo y su amor. Que Dios me los bendiga y me los protega. Los hecharé de menos, mamá y papá.*

Lib's voice cracks with the sentimentality of the Spanish and many of the faces in the crowd, including mine, get misty-eyed.

> And to CV High, we leave you, beloved home of our formative years, knowing that you are not perfect, but that you too will grow, and that you have learned from us as much as we have learned from you. Next year, you will be brighter and better, and so will the next generation of graduates who will be seated where we sit now.

The cheering seems to put a close to Lib's speech, but he doesn't leave the podium. Principal Beasley looks confused and Lib gives him the just-one-more-thing look.

Lib closes his valedictorian speech: "As a gesture of farewell, I'd like to ask all of the graduating seniors to lock their thumbs together and flutter their hands. Mariposa-style, we are off!"

Lib demonstrates. Not everyone in the group does it but there are enough who do, which makes it worth the effort. I look around to see if I can make eye contact with Trini, but I can't find her. It doesn't matter. I know she's definitely thinking the same thing I am at the moment: *Fierce!*

Another applause follows and the graduation ceremony continues with more speeches, the symbolic delivery of the diplomas, the final blessing and official certification, and the compulsory tossing of the mortar boards even though we were all warned not to do that because we might put someone's eye out.

As expected, many families end up having dinner at Las Cazuelas, but Mr. Benson has reserved the small banquet room just for the Mariposa Club. The Ramos family, the García family, the Gutiérrez family, the Simmons-Johnson family and Mr. Sandoval with Yolanda are gathered together for the first time in glorious mariposa harmony.

No more speeches are allowed, though there's plenty of toasting and all differences and tensions are put aside for the post-graduation festivities. Sheriff Johnson declares a truce with Sebastián, I declare a truce with Mr. Ramos, and Trini and Lib are in high spirits and avoid any unnecessary jabs. Mrs. Ramos is particularly pleased to be sitting next to Maddy, and they engage in a lively exchange, pregnant woman to pregnant woman.

For a minute I imagine that this is what world peace is like—margaritas and virgin daiquiris and the wonderful din of civility. But then, as a very frank reminder that we can't abandon reality for too long, Maddy lets out a conversation-halting screech. She starts going into labor.

Moving On

Call me sentimental, but the day after graduation and the birth of baby Robbie (who's a girl, by the way), I take a long walk. It's Sunday, but my work schedule's going to change for the summer as I officially take over for Yolanda on Monday. I hadn't planned on the walk. I simply wanted to step outside the door to get a sense of this new freedom. Now that I'm out of high school, is the air different? Is the sky? Not really. But I am. *I'm* different.

I step out into the driveway, and then farther out into the street, and the next thing I know I'm walking down the block, where I turn the corner and walk to the main boulevard that stretches across the entire town. I keep walking, past the dying dinosaur body of the Lame View Mall, past Trini's neighborhood, past the strip of boutiques downtown, where Amanda works, past Las Cazuelas and the row of fast-food restaurants that have been fattening generations of adolescents, until I arrive to Caliente Valley High School.

In the four years I attended this school, I've never been to the campus on a Sunday. The classrooms are locked, the pathways are empty, and even the planters, including the Queer Planter, look as if they're quite comfortable in their vacant states.

I want to walk inside, explore the sides of the walls, peek through the windows of the buildings—the administration office, the cafeteria, the gym. But I'd be trespassing. I no longer belong here. This is not my school anymore. Or my home.

So instead, I keep walking, past the high school buildings, past the athletic field and the parking lot. I cross the street into a neighborhood I have passed by many times over the years but have never been to. I don't know these houses or the people who live inside of them, I don't think, though I imagine a few of the high school students live here. But I don't know that. I walk along one of the streets and come across houses and doors and windows I have never seen before. I come across cars I may or may not have seen on the streets. This entire community has existed alongside mine for years and I am only now discovering it. I must get comfortable with this feeling of newness of experience and unfamiliarity. There will be many more days like it yet to come.

When I walk past the neighborhood, I reach a clearing in the desert and far off into the distance a road with cars that look no bigger than bugs. But instead of straining my eyes to see farther out, I take in my immediate surroundings: sand, rocks of varying textures and colors, mesquite, manzanita patches and wild crabgrass. I look closer: dandelions, verbena, buttercups and daisies. A whole world within my grasp.

But even here, in the familiar grounds, there's still room for surprise. From the corner of my eye, I catch something sputtering from the ground, straining to rise above this small kingdom.

Ah! A butterfly!

Rigoberto González

Acknowledgments

Thank you, once again, Steve Berman and Lethe Press/Tincture. Thank you, Corporation of Yaddo, for a timely residency in Saratoga Springs. And thank you to the readers of the Mariposa Club series for your kind words, your feedback and your fierceness.

Rigoberto González is the author of ten books of poetry and prose, and the editor of *Camino del Sol: Fifteen Years of Latina and Latino Writing*. The recipient of Guggenheim and NEA fellowships, winner of the American Book Award, and The Poetry Center Book Award, he writes a Latino book column for the *El Paso Times* of Texas. He is contributing editor for *Poets and Writers Magazine*, on the Board of Directors of the National Book Critics Circle, and is Associate Professor of English at Rutgers—Newark, State University of New Jersey.